DESERT ROSE

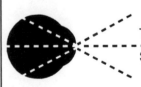

This Large Print Book carries the
Seal of Approval of N.A.V.H.

DESERT ROSE

COLLEEN L. REECE

THORNDIKE PRESS

An imprint of Thomson Gale, a part of The Thomson Corporation

THOMSON

™

GALE

Detroit • New York • San Francisco • New Haven, Conn. • Waterville, Maine • London

THOMSON

™

GALE

LIBRARY OF CONGRESS CATALOGING-IN-PUBLICATION DATA

Reece, Colleen L.
    Desert rose / by Colleen L. Reece.
      p. cm. — (Wildflower harvest series #2.) (Thorndike Press large print Christian romance)
      ISBN 0-7862-8902-3 (lg. print : alk. paper) 1. Large type books. I. Title.
PS3568.E3646D47 2006
813'.54—dc22   2006026994

U.S. Hardcover:
ISBN 13: 978-0-7862-8902-8
ISBN 10: 0-7862-8902-3

Published in 2006 by arrangement with Colleen L. Reece.

Printed in the United States of America on permanent paper
10 9 8 7 6 5 4 3 2 1

DESERT ROSE

ONE

Her auburn braid flying and brown eyes sparkling with determination, Desert Rose Birchfield reached her roan horse Mesquite and swung astride while her best friend and cousin Nate lagged a few steps behind. Five feet seven inches tall and 125 pounds, in the half-worn jeans she looked like a slim boy.

"Race you to the point!" Rose took advantage of her lead and touched Mesquite lightly with her boot heels.

"No fair!" Nate bellowed. He stepped into the stirrup and slid into Piebald's saddle. "You could give a fellow warning." He thundered behind the laughing girl. His dark hair tossed and his dark eyes, so like his father Nathaniel's and Uncle Adam's, glared at the lithe figure already a hundred yards ahead of him. With that kind of lead even faithful Piebald had little hope of catching Mesquite before they reached the bald knob overlooking the Double B ranch. The aerial vantage point provided a panoramic view of Wyoming's breathtaking Wind River Range.

By the time Nate dismounted Rose had already flung Mesquite's reins over his head so he would stand and thrown herself face down on a soft bed of pine needles. She rolled over and patted a fake yawn. "What took you so long?"

"One of these days . . ." Nate could never bring himself to list the dire consequences and Rose just laughed at him.

"Pooh, you know you can't get the best of me."

Her cousin dropped to the ground beside her, fingered a single pine needle, and tickled her bare arm with it. "I've been ahead of you ever since we were born, if you'll remember."

She indignantly sat up and her thick braid with the curl at the end flopped over her shoulder. A little candle of irritation lighted her dark brown eyes. "Just because you were born exactly one month ahead of me doesn't mean a thing."

"Dear child," he said pompously, pulling his mouth down. "Don't you know the Bible tells you to respect your elders?"

"As if that meant you," she scoffed and

moved out of his reach. "Why don't you go back to Concord, Massa-chew-sets, so we can have some peace again?" But Rose held her breath waiting for his reply. The past year that he had spent living out East with his paternal grandparents and attending school had been miserable, although she wouldn't tell him so.

"I'm not going back. Ever." Nate forgot his teasing and straightened to a crosslegged position. "Grandpa and Grandma Birchfield want me to live with them and study medicine but I can't."

"Why not? You — you don't want to be a minister like your father, do you?"

"And if I do?" He shot a searching glance at the cousin who was more like the sister he never had.

"Why —" She faltered as she felt her tanned cheeks redden. "You don't act like a minister. I mean, you'd have to be a lot different from what you are." She stopped, embarrassed and sorry when a hurt look crept into the dark eyes observing her so carefully. "Nate, are you *serious?*"

He didn't answer.

In desperation she babbled, "You don't have to decide now, do you? What does your father say? And Aunt Ivy?"

"They don't know anything about it. No

one does." Nate clenched his teeth and moodily stared out over the beautiful valley sheltered by saw-toothed mountains. "You aren't to say anything, either, Miss Smarty."

"As if I would. Have you ever known me to tell anything, especially anything you shared?"

"No." His short reply hung in the clear air. After a long silence Nate glanced at her. "As far as making up my mind, don't forget that we'll both be eighteen before 1893 is over." In a fluid movement, he stood and walked to the edge of the promontory. A magnificent eagle soared by above them. They could even distinguish the cattle that dotted the valley floor: Lazy H cattle owned by their friends, the Hardwicks; Double B cattle with the mingled ℬℬ brand that showed the twinship of Laurel and Ivy Brown who had married the Birchfield brothers. One section of land between the Lazy H and Double B ranches remained unsettled.

Rose came to Nate and slipped her arm through his. "I'm sorry I teased you," she whispered. "If God asks you to preach for Him, I know He will help you do it." When he didn't respond she added, "Do you — is — has God called you?" Funny how hard it was to discuss this new possibility. Never before had there been such constraint between them.

"That's the problem. I don't really know yet." The word *yet* rang a little bell inside Rose.

Nate's stumbling confession opened the floodgates and all his hesitancy vanished. "Sometimes I think it's just that I see the good Dad does, the way people say that he and your father have changed Antelope for the better in spite of all the trouble the past few years. Other times I know it's because of what Dad *is*. If I can be half the man he is, I'll be a success. Then once in a while when I'm riding alone at night the moonlight and mountains and foothills and trees shout that their Creator is present and that I must serve Him. I'm just not sure how. That's why I haven't said anything. This summer I have to make up my mind."

Rose felt as if her childhood companion had suddenly gone far away from her. She clutched Nate's arm. "Then why not enjoy this summer all you can and wait for God to help you know? Eighteen isn't so old."

Nate grinned the crooked grin that melted Rose every time. "That's what I thought until I went to Concord last year. Then I found out eighteen's a whole lot older out here than back there."

"Really? How?" Rose eagerly snatched at the subject, eager to rid that lost, little-boy look from Nate's face and the need to look at the future from her mind.

"Maybe it's because of all that's happened since we were born in 1875, or even before. How many times have we heard our folks and Grandpa and Grandma Brown tell how thousands of white people violated the Indian treaties and rushed into the Black Hills after gold was discovered in 1874?" Nate's face flushed with resentment and a sympathetic throb filled Rose's heart. Only too well did they know how the Indians held the Black Hills sacred and that the Sioux and Cheyenne tribes had retaliated. Peace in the summer of 1876 had been won at a terrible cost: At the Battle of the Little Bighorn, Sitting Bull, Crazy Horse, Gall, and others, along with 2000 Sioux warriors, the largest gathering in Western history, wiped out General George Armstrong Custer and his entire unit of over 200 soldiers.

"I don't blame the Indians," Rose declared. She clenched her shapely hands into fists. "If anyone tried to take our homes away from us or desecrate what we held sacred, I'd fight too."

"So would I," Nate agreed. "I feel sorry

for the Indians and I'm glad we haven't had trouble here."

"Have you seen Chief Running Deer since you came home?" Rose asked.

Nate shook his head. "No, but I will. Dad says he and his father Chief Grey Eagle proved themselves to be staunch friends years ago."

"My father always goes to take them medicine and never lets anyone know where their little tribe still lives," Rose put in. "They swore friendship before we were even born when Dad took Running Deer's appendix out and saved his life." She sighed. "I wish I could do something big and courageous like that. Not much chance here, though. Nate, I love Antelope but at times I feel I'll smother. Nothing ever happens."

"You ungrateful wretch!" Nate swung toward her, only half jesting. "What about oil being found in Wyoming in the early 80s? And you're certainly old enough to remember the winter of 1887!"

"Who could forget it?" she returned, feeling hot blood seep into her face. Rose tossed her braid and her exasperated grimace showed the tiny overlap of front teeth that lent pixie charm to her heart-shaped face.

"I'll never forget it as long as I live," Nate muttered.

Neither would Rose. Bitter temperatures and savage blizzards had killed thousands of cattle. Frozen corpses littered the valley and Thomas and Sadie Brown had been among the few to survive the ruin and hang on to their ranch. As the only doctor in the area, Rose's father Adam had been literally run off his feet; Uncle Nat had officiated at burials and comforted the sick, an equally demanding job.

Rose stirred restlessly. "I didn't mean *that* kind of thing."

"What did you mean?"

She stared at the tranquil scene below and focused on a tumbleweed idly moving but getting nowhere. "I don't know. I just feel that if I don't do something soon I'll explode like a bad jar of canning."

"Too bad you aren't more like Columbine," Nate teased.

"Columbine?" A vision of her brown-haired, brown-eyed coquettish sister shimmered in the heat waves before Rose's eyes. "That flirt? I heard Mother say she thanked God I took after her since Columbine's the spitting image of Ivy when she was fifteen."

Nate cocked his head to one side and smirked. "Granted Columbine's the flirtiest fifteen-year-old girl I've ever known, but just keep in mind how Aunt Laurel kicked over the family traces and rushed out here after Uncle Adam to get ahead of my mother!"

Before Rose could catch her breath he continued. "I just bet you wouldn't have the spunk to do something like that."

"Who says so?" Rose planted her hands on her hips and glared at him. Would she? *Perhaps,* she thought, *if I followed someone like Dad.*

"I do." Nate's natural lightheartedness and tendency to pester never stayed down long. A glint in his eyes struck fire to his volatile cousin. "Look, Rose Red —"

"Don't call me that. My hair is *not* red, it's auburn." She twitched the single heavy braid around for inspection.

"I could call you Roan Red. It's almost the same color as Mesquite." The quietly grazing horse lifted his head and nickered. Nate rolled on the ground with laughter. "Wonder if he's flattered?"

"You are so — so — I'm leaving." In a flash she had vaulted to the saddle with the barest touch of her toe to stirrup. "Come on, Mesquite."

"Hey, I'll come too." Nate sobered quickly and headed toward Piebald who showed signs of restiveness.

"Don't bother!" The words floated back over the girl's shoulder.

"I didn't mean to make you mad, Rosy."

"*Rose,* Nathaniel Birchfield the Second." There, that would get him. Nate hated being called his full name. If he insisted on being the bane of her life, he should get used to the thorns she could show.

Mesquite settled into the comfortable, rocking-chair gait that permitted his rider to dream while he did the work. Over the grassy slopes, still green from the unusual summer rains, the roan horse and auburn-haired girl seemed to move as one. From the back of Piebald Nate observed how much taller she had grown in the year he spent back East. At five feet ten inches and still growing he could look down on her but deep inside he knew he also looked up to the beautiful girl. *Would he ever find a girl to match her?*

"God willing," he muttered. "And that she finds someone who will be worthy of her." He frowned until his black brows met above the dark eyes that could change from laughter to deep thought so quickly. "There's not a man on the range who is good enough for her," he told Piebald in a voice too low to carry to the girl ahead. "In fact, I've only known one man outside of Dad and Uncle

Adam who could handle her with love and the firm hand she's going to need." His mouth twitched. "Herein is a matchmaker born, but how?"

For several days Nate put aside his own weighty considerations and plotted. Over 2000 miles lay between Wyoming and Massachusetts. Besides, if Rose were allowed to go to school back East, what guarantee had anyone that she wouldn't follow her headstrong ways and fall in love with some rotter? Living in a so-called civilized part of the country didn't ensure ideals and morality. Nate had found as many scoundrels in his year in Concord as in Antelope. They wore finer clothes and looked down their haughty noses at westerners, but Nate's keen vision penetrated to their core. He couldn't take a chance on a bedazzled Rose getting tangled up with a skunk in Harvard clothing!

Perhaps he should go back with her. Yet not even for Rosy would he endure another year in a strange land. He had studied hard and proved himself, but he had counted the months, weeks, and days until he could come home. The same restless, seeking spirit that had lured his father and uncle to the frontier more than twenty years earlier ran strong in Nate's veins.

Did he dare pray about his scheme? If he prayed and God said no, that would be it. Better to simply set the stage and let God take over at that point, he assured his conscience. He did relent enough to say, "Dear God, You know how much I think of Rose and I do have her best interests at heart. All I want her to do is have the chance to meet him. Then it will be up to You." No lightning flash or thunderclap came so Nate quickly added, "Amen," and rode off to find Rose, determined to wait and watch for the perfect opportunity.

He almost missed it when it presented itself the next day. He came down the stairs of the Double B to find Columbine and Rose giggling over a magazine they hastily stuffed under a pillow when he entered.

"What's this?" Nate pounced and withdrew a copy of *Hand and Heart.* He disgustedly tossed it aside. "What are you two doing reading this, anyway?"

"There's nothing wrong with it," Columbine defended in her haughtiest southern belle fashion. "Why shouldn't people advertise for wives and husbands?" She dissolved in laughter again.

"Some of them are hilarious." Rose wiped her eyes and snatched the magazine back. "Listen to this 'Wanted: Wife to cook, bake, and sew. No ridin', ropin', or brandin'.' "

"That's not in there!" Nate peered over her shoulder.

"It sure is. This one's even better. 'You kin have yore own stove, you kin have yore own pony. Wyomin' winters git mighty lonely.' Here's another. 'Young, healthy female wants to keep company with strong, healthy rancher. Object: matrimony.' Oh dear, do you think anyone ever answers these?"

"You bet they do." Columbine suddenly dropped her affected air. "Mrs. Hardwick said her own sister answered an ad in a magazine like this only it was called *Heart and Ring* and she married the advertiser and they've been happy for over twenty years!" She shivered and the mischief faded from her pretty face. "A girl would be taking an awful chance, though."

"She sure would. She might get someone like Nate," Rose tormented.

Nate didn't say a word. An idea had popped full-blown into his fertile brain. "How about a ride, Rose?"

"I'll be ready by the time you saddle Mesquite for me," she told him and ran to change her clothes.

"May I go too?" Columbine asked.

"Not this time." Nate barely saw the

disconsolate droop of her lips. "Sam will be out later." He knew his sixteen-year-old brother adored Columbine and never had been able to understand why they didn't get along the way he and Rose did.

"Oh, Sam." Columbine drifted away, leaving Nate feeling uncomfortable. Someday he would include her but not today, not when he held the means to carry out his plan concerning Rose.

No matter which direction they rode, Nate and Rose almost always ended up on the point. They never tired of the changing sky, the slight breeze there on most days, and the feeling of solitude.

Today they mutually turned Mesquite and Piebald toward the flower-strewn slopes and came out on the bluff that ended in the bald knob viewpoint. As usual, Mesquite and Piebald grazed with reins hanging loose.

"Red Rose, Roan Rose, Rosy, what kind of man do you want to marry?"

Nate's question burst a moment of absolute silence. Rose turned her astonished gaze toward Nate. "Whatever makes you ask that?"

"Most people get married when they're younger than we are," he reminded her. "We haven't talked about it for ages, but you used to say you wanted someone to ride straight out of a storybook. Come on. Who's your hero now?"

She hesitated so long he looked at her closely and followed the line of her watching eyes to the distant mountain peaks. "Someone strong and gentle like Dad and Uncle Nat."

Nate's heart leaped. He thought of his candidate for Rose's hand. *So far, so good.*

"And?"

"He has to love God above anything, even me."

Nate leaned closer to catch the final two words. "Is that all?"

Rose abandoned her seriousness. "Of course not. He has to be rich and exciting and handsome and . . . why are you looking at me like that?" she demanded.

"I'm just wondering if you have the courage to do something really exciting and new, something you've never done before and will never do again." He laughed until his white teeth gleamed in the sunlight against his tanned, handsome face.

"I have the courage to do anything you can think up," she said rashly.

"Promise? You're a scaredy cat if you don't," he taunted. He saw her hesitate and he pushed his advantage. "I knew you wouldn't do it."

21

"I will," she flashed, all imperiousness and determination.

Nate pulled the crumpled issue of *Hand and Heart* out from under his shirt where he'd stashed it. "I dare you to send an advertisement to them."

Rose's hand flew to her mouth. Her eyes looked enormous. "Dad would kill me. So would Mother."

"How will they know? How many *Hand and Heart* copies have you ever seen?"

"None," she admitted. "Columbine brought it home from visiting in Rock Springs."

"Well?" Nate held his breath, counting on her well-known unwillingness to let him get the best of her and pushing back the thought this wasn't fair.

"All right." But she sighed. "I don't know why I let you get me into pickles all the time and this will probably be another one but I said I would and I'll do it. Why don't *you* send one?"

Nate had already prepared himself for that question. "Too much competition. Anyway, there are hardly any from girls. You're sure to get answers." *At least one,* he promised himself.

An hour later an announcement more

exaggerated than any in *Hand and Heart* had been composed. "I'll write it out and send it," Nate promised. "That way there's less chance of your getting caught." That night he kept part of his bargain. He copied and mailed the advertisement and sent a picture, but *not* to *Hand and Heart*.

Two

Carmichael Blake-Jones stared at the ivy-covered walls that had held him ever since he graduated from college and began teaching. The late afternoon sunlight that turned the stone walls rosy flickered in his curly golden hair and reduced his twenty-three years until he looked more like one of the boys who came to the private school than an instructor. A pang of regret slipped through him. *Had he been insane to give up this privileged teaching post? Had the whim of a moment resulted in folly?*

He could go back into the dean's office and retract his resignation. Yet Carmichael hesitated and the moment passed. He turned on his heel and walked away, only pausing at the stone-arched gates to look back.

An imaginary parade of teenage boys marched between him and the school. Tall, short, overweight, underweight, timid, bold, good, and mischievous, he had loved many, despised a few for their cowardice or cheating, but served all. His fun-loving personality sympathized with their dilemmas and he had often been hard put to keep from laughing instead of meting out the necessary discipline. Even the boys who thought him a pushover on first acquaintance soon learned that B. J., as they called him, offered friendship as well as education but never allowed himself to be maneuvered.

Now his new freedom sat heavily on his broad shoulders. *What next?*

The unspoken challenge echoed in every footstep between the school and his ancestral home. Born and raised in Concord, "one of those dyed-in-the-wool New Englanders," a fellow teacher had labeled him, Carmichael loved his home. And yet. . . . He tossed his head back and laughed aloud. If that teacher and the others only knew! How often in dreams had the dedicated teacher longed to step from the rut he could feel growing deeper and more comfortable daily — to strike out and travel, to search for more adventure than he could find here.

Carmichael automatically returned greetings from those who hailed him, left the business district, and walked on, glad for the considerable distance between home and the school. In bad weather the walk had proved inconvenient but on an early summer day with a beckoning sun spilling its joy Carmichael was unaware of the distance. His steps dragged, however, when he came to the corner of the Blake-Jones property. Not large enough to be called an estate, the spacious grounds and solid brick home showed the permanence of long standing. Sparkling white columns gave the mellowed brick a clean and welcoming look. Carmichael sighed. In the weeks since his parents had been killed in a railway accident he hated coming home. The youngest of the children and able to live at home long after the others had married and gone, a special bond had strengthened between him and his parents.

The mouth that stayed etched in a smile twisted bitterly. Since the accident Carmichael had been bereft of even his Heavenly Father's comfort. A dozen times he had cried out, "Why, God? They loved and served You. You could have protected them. Why didn't you?" Only the high ceilings replied, with silence. At last his prayers dwindled to formal recognition and he suffered alone.

"Michael, is that you?" a girlish voice called from the top of the curving staircase that led to the second floor.

His heart lifted. "Here. What are you up to?"

Sixteen-year-old Mercy Curtis pelted downstairs, her skirts clutched with one hand to keep her from tripping. Plump and just a little over five feet tall, she wore her gold curls so like her mother Caroline's and Uncle Carmichael's in a topknot that threatened to topple at any moment. Her blueberry blue eyes twinkled. "I've come to take care of you, of course."

"You have *what?*" Long familiar with her impetuous actions, her blunt announcement still surprised him while her warm hug took away some of his emptiness.

"You know I'm as good a cook as Mandy and can keep house a whole lot better. I just told Mama and Daddy that it didn't make sense for you to be rattling around all alone in this ark, excuse me, house —" She paused to grin and her teeth flashed against the healthy red lips. "Anyway, now that school is out I don't have anything to do except help Mama, so here I am."

For the second time this afternoon Carmichael laughed spontaneously. Mercy had dressed for the part by adding one of Mandy's voluminous aprons over her gingham dress and wrapping it around herself

27

twice. She wore a cap whose origins looked suspiciously like a dish towel. Now she bobbed a little curtsy and assumed a meek expression that her twin dimples somehow defeated. "Will Master Michael be ready for his tea in five minutes?" In her own voice, she added, "He'd better. I helped Mandy make popovers and they'll fall if you don't hurry."

Still laughing, Carmichael sped upstairs, hastily washed, and arrived at the tea table where the popovers sat puffed and waiting. For the first time in weeks he actually enjoyed a meal. Having Mercy there did make a difference. "Now, young lady," he began when they finished the light meal, "you aren't serious, are you?"

Her blue eyes opened wide. "Of course I am. Once I convinced Mama it would be good training for me to have charge of a house because I'll be getting married one of these days —"

"Married!" He set down his teacup with a little crash that brought a cry of dismay from Mercy until she saw it hadn't cracked. "Why, you're still a baby!"

"Oh?" Red flags of color flared in her face but her voice stayed sweet. "Let me run this house for one month and you'll see how much of a baby I am." She fixed him with a stern stare. "In case you've forgotten, I am almost seventeen years old."

Delighted at her reaction, he added, "Your birthday isn't until December."

She hurriedly changed the subject. "Can I stay?"

He wasn't to be sidetracked. "Just who do you have in mind to marry, that you need this practice?"

"How should I know?" She shrugged her plump shoulders and grinned again. "Your school's filled with boys, isn't it? I thought maybe you could pick out a few of the extra nice ones. Oh!" She jumped up so quickly the little tea table rocked. "You got a letter." She ran to the mantel and brought back a fat envelope then perched on the arm of his chair and peered over his shoulder. "Nathaniel Birchfield. Isn't he that boy who went to your school last year?" An undercurrent of excitement pinkened her smooth face.

Carmichael eyed her suspiciously. "How do you happen to remember him? I don't think I ever introduced you."

"You didn't have to. He came to church with his grandparents. He was — different. Sort of nice different."

Totally amused but intrigued, he let the letter lie unopened on the table. "What do you mean by that, Mercy?"

She traced the damask pattern on the tablecloth with her forefinger. "He just smiled and didn't act smart or try to flirt."

"Well, I would certainly hope not," Carmichael retorted. "Nice young gentlemen don't flirt with little girls." Storm warnings in his niece's eyes made him add, "After all, last year you were only fifteen and didn't even have your hair up."

She relaxed and smiled. "Aren't you going to open your letter?"

Carmichael scowled. "If you take over as housekeeper, you are going to have to learn your place and not show such vulgar curiosity about the Master's mail." But he hugged her and smiled then slit open the letter. A flat, tissue-wrapped card fell out and to the floor.

"I'll get it." Mercy swooped off the arm of the chair and scooped it up. The wrapping fell back. "Why, it's a photograph!" She stared. "Uncle Michael, have you been keeping secrets?"

Carmichael grabbed the photograph and gasped. A girl mounted on a fine-looking horse smiled back at him. A long, thick braid with a curl on the end hung over her shoulder. The likeness had caught sparkling eyes and a wide, white smile. Dressed for riding, she was clad in boys' jeans and a long-sleeved shirt.

"Who is she?" Mercy demanded.

"I have no idea." Carmichael couldn't take his gaze from the picture.

"She's beautiful. No, not exactly, but better than pretty," Mercy judged. "She looks like she'd be fun and see the way she sits her horse. Oh, if Mama would let me ride in pants! I hate riding in skirts, they bundle so."

Carmichael's keen eyes caught the rearing mountains in the background and he turned toward the letter. "I wonder why Nate Birchfield sent this picture? Perhaps he put it in by mistake."

"Read it and find out," Mercy said practically and resumed her seat on his chair arm, avidly following Nate's letter.

Antelope, Wyoming
June 1893

Dear Mr. Blake-Jones,

You probably didn't think you'd ever hear from me once I got back home. I'm not coming back to Concord, as I told you when I left. I learned so much from you, but now it's time to move on and out here in the West is where I belong.

I want to thank you for everything you

31

did for me and I will write again after I decide what to do with my life. I'm taking this summer to consider and I just may have surprising news for you a little later. In the meantime, I wonder if you'd do a favor for me. It's this way.

My cousin Desert Rose Birchfield is always trying to get ahead of me and she usually does! Now I have a chance to have some harmless fun if you'll help. I talked her into writing an advertisement for *Hand and Heart* magazine, the one where people advertise for wives and sometimes husbands. . . ."

Mercy interrupted with a little scream. "My stars, how did she have the nerve?"

"If you *have* to read my mail, kindly refrain from commenting on it," Carmichael told her, tipping the page so she couldn't see it. As usual with Mercy he relented and read aloud.

Now, fun is one thing but having someone answer who will get angry when she turns him down — as she will — or even worse, someone who will hang around her wouldn't be funny at all. Besides, her parents and mine would lambaste us for doing this.

Anyway, I just thought that you might write her a letter. She probably won't ever answer or, if she does, you can stop corresponding at any time and she'll think you lost interest. I am enclosing a picture of Rose and her letter to *Hand and Heart* and will be much obliged if you will at least write one time.

Respectfully yours,
Nathaniel "Nate" Birchfield II

P.S. If you write, please don't tell her how you got her advertisement.

"Of all the ridiculous requests!" Carmichael dropped the letter to the table.

"*I* think it's perfectly splendid," Mercy cried. She caught the single sheet of paper that had drifted out and laid it to one side. "Will you read Desert Rose Birchfield's advertisement or shall I? Oh, what a pretty name!" All eagerness, her greedy fingers unfolded the page but she waited for Carmichael's permission.

"Go ahead." He leaned back in his chair and feigned indifference even while he glanced again at the laughing girl in the photograph. Desert Rose. Her name suited her.

"Just listen!" Mercy giggled until he couldn't understand her. In exasperation,

Carmichael took the advertisement from her.

Wanted: Young man to correspond with almost-eighteen-year-old girl.

"I wonder when *her* birthday is," Carmichael broke off to say.
"Go on!" Mercy ordered.

Must be at least five foot ten, have sense of humor, faith in God, be willing to relocate in Wyoming should correspondence lead to a closer companionship. No drinkers, smokers, or dandies. Must have good education but not be stuffy, no younger than twenty or older than twenty-five. Financial stability required. No ranching experience necessary, but must love horses and be willing to learn range lore. The ability to adapt to scorching and freezing temperatures, blizzards and droughts, hailstorms, and gully-washers mandatory. Must be good-natured and not easily provoked. No divorced men or widowers need write. Will exchange photographs only after advertiser determines it worthwhile.

"Is that all?" Mercy tried to see the page.

"What more do you want?" her uncle demanded. "You can see that this Rose deliberately made up an impossible person in order to best Nate." He tossed the advertisement to the table.

Mercy immediately took possession of it. A golden curl fell over her forehead as she perused it. "Hmmm. You're exactly five foot ten, have a sense of humor, faith in God —"

"For goodness sake, Mercy! Stop your foolishness." But Carmichael had all he could do not to show curiosity as she ignored him and rattled on.

"You don't drink or smoke and you're the right age. Now that you've inherited a tidy sum from Grandpa and Grandma you are financially stable. You aren't a dandy and haven't been married and I'd hate to see you go to Wyoming but you could adapt if you had to and you love horses and already ride well. You're good natured, at least when you get your own way, and, why Uncle Michael! You're everything Desert Rose made up!" She stared at him admiringly. "May I read your letter to her?" Mercy's eyes shone with plans and dreams. "What if you write and she answers and you fall in love? You could use your inheritance to buy a ranch in Wyoming and I'll come out and keep house for you until I find a cowboy who'll carry me off on his horse and marry me and we'll all live happily ever after!"

Why should a wild leap of excitement shoot through him at his niece's nonsense? For a single moment her eloquence had swayed him. Common sense came to Carmichael's rescue. "I thought you said you were grown up enough to run a home? This kind of talk certainly proves how wrong you are," he said sarcastically. "I have no intention of getting involved in a childish prank."

Mercy's dismay seemed out of proportion to his decision. Her blue eyes darkened. "You mean you won't answer? But you have to! What if you don't? Desert Rose will think no one likes her well enough to correspond. She will feel absolutely terrible." Mercy dramatically pointed to the photograph. "You can't be so mean you won't write just one little letter to her! I know how I would feel if I never got a reply." She managed a woebegone expression that sent Carmichael into fits of laughter.

Mercy seized her advantage. "Just one letter, Michael?" she pleaded.

"I'll consider it." He shut his lips tight in the way that warned the subject had been closed.

Mercy said no more — then. But in the

days following after Carmichael and the girl's parents agreed the responsibility of housekeeping might do Mercy good, she quietly began a campaign that made the most illustrious army general look like an enlistee. Innocent little phrases such as, "Desert Rose will start looking for a letter soon" crept into her conversation. Now and then she sighed, "I wonder if Desert Rose would like to have me write to her? No, that would spoil Nate's plan."

Finally Carmichael capitulated, aware of how the simple photograph propped on the mantel (where Mercy placed it) drew his attention each time he entered the well-kept, comfortable room. "All right, I'll write tonight."

"Good!" His tormentor became his ally and clapped her hands in victory. Never had her eyes glowed more like sapphires and Carmichael recognized a startling truth. His not-yet-seventeen-year-old niece indeed trembled on the brink of womanhood. In spite of her small stature, Mercy no longer could be considered a child. Even Mandy admitted it.

On one point he held firm against her half-pouting pleas. "No, you may *not* read my letter. In the first place, all I'm going to do is tell her the truth — that I've been a teacher at a private boys' school and am in the process of making some changes in my life."

"Are you going to tell her you know Nate?"

He drew his brows into a straight line and a rueful smile played on his lips. "I think I'll have to. She's bound to discover it or ask Nathaniel."

Long after Mercy slept in the guest room she had appropriated, the one with the canopy bed she had always adored, Carmichael struggled with his letter. He wrote and discarded a dozen letters and finally settled on a simple message based on the outline he had sketched for Mercy's benefit. His golden curls grew damp with effort. His blue eyes brightened and dulled in turn. At last his sense of humor won over the feeling he wasn't being quite square with the girl who wore the odd name Desert Rose so well.

He sealed the envelope, exhilarated yet half-disgusted with himself. An hour later he lay wide-eyed and sleepless. Tales Nate had shared with the teacher who had seen through his bravado to find a homesick but determined young man crept into Carmichael's thoughts. Never once had he felt Nate exaggerated.

"He didn't have to!" Carmichael whispered and chuckled. The Old West and its fight against the elements certainly hadn't faded into history. Just living and winning in Wyoming could challenge a man or a woman to the utmost.

What was she like, the young woman in the picture? Obviously as filled with a love of fun as her cousin Nathaniel. She must also possess a tremendous faith or she wouldn't have included that in her ridiculous advertisement. Something in her eyes showed innocence wedded to mischief, the same traits Caroline once said her younger brother Carmichael possessed.

Surely suitors flocked around Desert Rose. For some strange reason Carmichael resented the thought then wondered why. Yet, knowing one Birchfield as he did, and judging from Desert Rose's advertisement, he'd bet not a man in a hundred would so much as carelessly attempt a caress.

Carmichael jerked upright in bed, appalled at his train of thought. Good heavens, if just writing a letter to Nate's cousin affected him like this he'd best tear up the letter and write to Nate in no uncertain terms that he disapproved of the whole scheme and would have no part in it.

He tossed and turned and awakened more

determined than ever to retrieve the letter from his desk in the writing room and replace it with a scorching missive to Nate. Tired, out of sorts, and thoroughly ashamed of his weakening before Mercy's assault, Carmichael dressed and strode down to the writing room.

The desk lay empty.

"Mercy?" he called, his heart thumping.

"Here," came the answer from the hall. "I just ran out and got your letter posted."

THREE

To Carmichael's amazement, Mercy turned out to be capable and thrifty in running his household. Mandy, who had felt without direction since the elder master and mistress died, gave thanks and sang Mercy's praises. "I can cook most anything that's fried, baked, boiled, or stewed," she stated, "but I needs someone to tell me what they want cooked." She added a little forlornly, "Master Michael, you just ain't so good at that."

He sighed, thinking of his lack of interest in food the past months, but his eyes brightened and he patted faithful Mandy's arm. "You won't let Mercy boss you, will you?"

"Land sakes, why would she do that?" Mandy settled into her favorite pose, her arms akimbo. "We works together. Like two hands on one person."

Carmichael's keen observance confirmed Mandy's claim. The girl-woman and the old cook complemented each other and the household machinery never creaked under their joint efforts.

To Carmichael, Mercy's abnormal curiosity and romantic views were the only thorns in his life. Long before the letter to Wyoming could have reached its destination Mercy haunted the post for an answer. Her uncle laughed at her until his blue eyes crinkled at the corners. "You don't honestly think she'll reply, do you? Writing to such a magazine on a dare is a far cry from actually responding to an unknown man over 2000 miles away."

Mercy's round chin set stubbornly. "She'll answer. Any girl with Desert Rose's spunk is bound to. *I* would," she belligerently added.

"I don't doubt that!" her long-suffering uncle agreed. He clasped his hands behind his head and looked at his pretty companion. How nice to have someone across the table at meals! To hear singing while Mercy cleaned and dusted and proved how well trained she had been by her conscientious mother. Carmichael knew he had always avoided girls, especially those who showed eagerness for his company. Having sisters so much older than himself had been a disadvantage. He didn't feel comfortable around giggling girls. Teaching at the boys' school had only compounded the problem. He never had difficulty dealing with mothers but his situation offered little opportunity to meet the opposite sex. Besides, his studies and work had absorbed him. Someday he'd marry, but with the comfortable home his mother provided he had been lazy about pursuing such a relationship. Only since living in the big and empty house alone had Carmichael realized how much he missed the presence of others. Once he suggested that Mandy eat with him but she had thrown her apron over her head.

"It ain't proper," she announced.

He hadn't pursued the idea. Now Mercy filled a gap he hadn't even known existed until recently. It made all the difference in the world to come downstairs and see his plump niece tucked into a chair, her pretty hands busy with needlework or mending.

One evening he told her, "You really are going to make a good wife someday."

Her silver knitting needles slowed and her dimples appeared. "I know."

He laughed the joyous laugh that had returned with her arrival. "Of all the smug and complacent girls, you're the worst."

"Why?" She dropped her half-knitted sweater and squared off. "Don't you know that you're a good teacher?"

"Of course I do." He had the grace to turn red and grin weakly, thinking what an attractive picture she made in her simple pink dress with something white and frothy at the neckline.

"Uncle Michael, what are you going to do at the end of summer? I still have a year of school at least. Mother and Daddy want me to go to college — can you beat that? Me, in college!"

He couldn't help teasing. "From the sound of your grammar, college wouldn't hurt you."

Her laughing blue eyes darkened. "Don't change the subject." Concern showed in every line of her body.

Carmichael respected that concern and answered accordingly after staring out the window into the summer dusk. The heavy scent of night-blooming flowers drifted in to color the conversation. Night birds crying sent a pang of loneliness through the young man at a crossroads. "I don't know, Mercy," he told her quietly, speaking as if to a contemporary rather than a girl. "Now that I'm alone I don't relish the thought of staying here. That's why I resigned." He felt her stir but she remained silent, perhaps from shock. He hadn't even told Mandy about his resignation.

"You laughingly said a few days ago I could sell this place and go buy a ranch out West. At first I laughed at the idea. . . ." His voice trailed into the twilight.

"And now?" Mercy leaned forward and kept her voice low.

"It isn't such a bad idea." In a wave of companionship he opened up hopes and dreams he had never shared with anyone but God. "I love Concord and all it stands for but something inside me cries out for adventure. What am I doing here spending my time teaching mostly sons of rich parents who will send them to all the places I long to see? I have the money to travel, to see and do and go. Once I marry, what chance will there be for me to experience foreign places or the West or a hundred other things?" His well-shod feet paced the costly Oriental rug.

"I also wonder if I could succeed in a place where I am not known and accepted because of our long line of worthy ancestors. You know what I'd really like to do? Go somewhere and work with my hands. Sweat and become exhausted and know hunger and cold. If I could find a place that requires manhood and hard work, I'd leave Concord tomorrow!" His eyes glowed and he could feel excitement surge through his entire body.

Mercy stared at him. He saw how her face gleamed in the deepening dusk. "Then go, Michael. Don't let anyone stop you." The glitter of tears in her tangled lashes confirmed how much she meant every word. "If I were a little older or a young man, I'd go with you." A small smile hovered on her lips. "Remember Desert Rose's description of Wyoming? It sounds an awful lot like the place you described."

Blood rushed to Carmichael's head. The feelings he had denied ever since looking at the jutting mountain background against which Desert Rose Birchfield so easily sat her mount returned in full force. "Who would hire anyone like me in a country like that?"

Some of Mercy's usual dreaming joined with her New England practicality. She impatiently brushed away her tears. "If you owned a ranch you'd have a job just as you said you wanted." She jumped up and hugged him. "Will you let me come out as soon as I finish school next spring?"

"Whoa!" His arms tightened around the niece he had really only discovered in the last few weeks. "You're going too fast for me." Yet he thrilled at the pictures that frolicked in his mind. Away from everything he knew, among new people, facing a new land, might he lose the anger he held toward his Heavenly Father for not intervening and saving his parents? If mountain peaks, rolling hills, and green valleys could offer healing to his spirit and a return to his childhood faith, any amount of money would be well spent.

For hours they sat up talking until even Mercy couldn't keep her eyes open. The next day they continued their conversation, weighing and considering. Finally they decided Carmichael should write, not to Desert Rose, but to Nathaniel Birchfield II, casually inquiring about the availability of small ranches in the area near Antelope. The letter would contain a strict warning for Nate to say nothing to anyone concerning Carmichael's questions.

A reply arrived in record time. Nate obviously had hopped on his horse and thoroughly researched every ranch within miles. Carmichael could picture the eager young man who stood as tall as his former teacher interviewing various cowmen, his hat shoved back on his forehead, his dark eyes giving nothing away. Nate's enthusiasm was evident.

There isn't a lot for sale but what there

47

is will knock your eyes out. I had no idea Old Man Turpin wanted to sell out and go live with his daughter in Rock Springs. The Circle 5 is a pretty little spread that could be made into a paying proposition if a man had the money to do it. The house and outbuildings are a little rundown. I guess since Mrs. Turpin died, the old man hasn't cared enough to keep them up. Besides, he doesn't look too well.

There are only a couple of hundred cattle but the range will hold many more. The spread is quite a ways from Antelope but not so far from Grandpa and Grandma Brown's Double B ranch.

Are you serious or just asking? So far nobody but I knows the ranch is for sale but news like that leaks out fast. You won't have any trouble getting good hands and the view's grand. A dandy trout stream runs through the upper part of the property and there's enough timber to build a dozen ranchhouses. Besides, you'll have great neighbors! *Let me know pronto* if you're interested and send along a few bucks to hold the deal until you can get here.

Nate had scrawled his name below and sketched in a crude drawing of what must be the Circle 5. On one ferocious looking critter that must be a bull he had drawn the Circle 5 brand. The miniature ⑤ that held Carmichael's attention seemed to draw the disapproving looks of all his New England ancestors pictured in gold frames around the living room.

"Are you going to buy it?" Mercy hung over her uncle's shoulder in her favorite position for inspecting his mail. She took a long breath. "If you do, I want Indian rugs on the walls of my room and a soft bed and two windows overlooking that." She pointed to the rough portrayal of rolling hills that rose to serrated peaks.

"Your room? My dear young woman, how you run on."

She smiled her bewitching smile that so often won whatever she wanted. "You'll be busy at first but you have almost a year to get your log house built and you may as well know before you start how I want my room to be."

He threw up his hands at her daring. "The idea. Why, you're ready to move into an imaginary bedroom in a house that isn't and may never be built on a ranch I don't own!"

Unfazed, she merely reached for the sketch and began making outlandish suggestions for a house of lodge proportions that any Astor or Vanderbilt would be proud to occupy.

Mercy received more fuel to add to her growing fire of reasons why her favorite uncle should go West. The morning post brought a squeal from the excitable girl and put her more practical uncle in shock.

Desert Rose had answered Carmichael's letter.

He could hardly believe his own eyes when he saw his name and address in a clear, firm handwriting that had no "feminine" swirls. He could see that Mercy itched to tear open the letter but a newborn loyalty to the girl in the picture made him say, "It wouldn't be fair for me to let you read it."

She looked so downcast he quickly added, "I'll tell you what she says, though."

"Good." Mercy settled herself in a nearby chair and Carmichael could feel her eyes boring into him as he read. Unwilling to keep her in suspense too long, he skimmed each paragraph and condensed its contents.

"She's quite surprised that anyone so far away would run across her advertisement. She says she hadn't realized that *Hand and Heart* would ever penetrate the august walls of a private boys' school."

Mercy giggled and her eyes flashed. "What else?"

"Oh, she says she asked Nate about me and he assured her that it's safe to correspond, that I'm not the kind of man who would take advantage of her letters or would bother her." Carmichael exploded. "Confound the rascal! I'll bet he's laughing behind both of our backs."

"Don't stop there," his niece begged, sitting on the edge of her chair.

"She says it's kind of me to write and that she appreciates the opportunity to learn more about the East than her parents and Nate have told her and that —" He stopped reading but his gaze traveled on.

Mercy couldn't restrain herself. "What does she say? What does she *say?*" She bounced up and down despite the danger of falling off her chair.

Carmichael couldn't keep back his grin. He folded the letter and put it back into the envelope. "Just that if I ever decide to visit Nate, all the Birchfields will welcome me." He didn't repeat the final part of the last sentence: *Nate speaks highly of you and I am thankful that you are the one to answer my advertisement.*

Mercy crossed her arms and looked at him suspiciously. Carmichael maintained an expression of bland innocence to match her own and diverted further questions. "I think

I'll write to Nate and send those 'bucks' he talked about. Even if I don't decide to become a cattle rancher this Circle 5 sounds like a good investment."

"I agree. As your friend Nate said, you'll have such nice neighbors." With this parting shot Mercy ran toward the kitchen. "It must be time for lunch and I'm starved." She paused in the doorway and mischief surrounded her like a halo. "Better eat civilized food while you can, Uncle dear. If things get tough in Wyoming you may end up dining on rattlesnake and prairie dogs." A smothered laugh later, she disappeared.

"Good little scout," Carmichael said out loud. Mercy had kept quiet about his affairs and even Mandy didn't know all the possibilities floating around the Blake-Jones home.

Carmichael's half-formed determination to buy the Circle 5 wavered when he suddenly thought of Mandy. Could Caroline and her husband take her? Never, ever would she be turned out after the decades of service to "her family." Widowed and childless, she had come to them while still a young woman and had grown old caring for the different children. "Dear God," he whispered, "is this all some ridiculous plan to escape everything here, even me? Or is it something You want for me?"

For the first time since the double funeral Carmichael Blake-Jones felt a little warmth stir in his frozen heart. He quickly added, "Please, help me know. . . ."

Letters raced between Massachusetts and Wyoming. The price Old Man Turpin was asking for the Circle 5 was both fair and sensible, Nate wrote. His investigation and knowledge of Wyoming land values confirmed it. More and more Carmichael picked up Mercy's trick of saying, "When I get to Wyoming" rather than "If I go." At last he finally faced the last hurdle.

Mercy's usual quick understanding caught the frustration in his voice one day while he raised various objections. Suddenly she burst out, "By the way, if you're worrying about Mandy, don't. I asked Mother and Daddy a week ago if we could have her in case you ever decided to teach somewhere else. Mother clasped her hands and looked like I'd offered her a good-sized chunk of heaven."

Mercy mimicked Caroline perfectly. " 'Having Mandy here would mean free time for me to read and maybe even gad a bit, especially now that Mercy has been working with her. I could turn the house-work and cooking over to them and be a lady of leisure.' "

"I wonder how Mandy would feel?" Carmichael dreaded even bringing it up with their faithful friend.

"Want me to find out?" Mercy offered. Her eyes narrowed and she tapped her lips with one finger.

"Would you? Can you, without giving anything away?"

"Just watch me." She raised her voice and called, "Mandy, could you come in here for a moment, please?"

Carmichael held his breath while Mandy entered and perched on the chair Mercy indicated.

"Mandy, I can't bear the thought of having to go home when Uncle Michael doesn't need me any longer. We've had such fun and you've taught me so much."

Her wistful voice and eyes told Carmichael how sincere Mercy really was and brought a wide smile to Mandy's face. Mercy continued, twisting her handkerchief but keeping her blue gaze on Mandy. "Would you ever consider coming to live with us? I mean, if Uncle Michael didn't need you any more?"

Mandy solemnly stared at her then at Carmichael. "It'd be pure joy being with Miss Car'line and you, child." She turned a longing look at the teasing girl. "I reckon if ever Michael takes him a wife he could spare me."

A great load fell from Carmichael. He impulsively crossed the room, knelt at the old woman's side, and took her worn hands in his. "Mandy, I'm not taking a wife but I am seriously considering going away from Concord."

"It's a mighty good thing, Master Michael." Mandy smiled when his mouth dropped open. "This place ain't really home now that Master and Missus are gone to heaven. I been expecting this. Don't you worry none over old Mandy." She beamed at Mercy. "That child will warm my heart just as you did."

A thought made Carmichael ask, "Suppose I got a home somewhere else, a long way off, maybe. Would you come, as far as Wyoming, maybe?"

Mandy considered for a long while. Then her lined face brightened. "I reckon it would depend on who needed me the most, you or Miss Car'line and this here child."

"You know you'll always be part of our family no matter what," Mercy put in. She bounded over to hug Mandy. "We'll have the best time. I can just hear Mother singing praises when we take over her work so she can rest."

With the final problem overcome, Carmichael succumbed to the lure of the West. He and Mercy decided that he should not tell Desert Rose who he was when he reached Antelope. "She'd think you raced out there post-haste and it might spoil everything," Mercy wisely pointed out. She frowned then her face cleared. "I know. Tell her you'll be traveling and to send her letters in care of me. No, that's not so good. She might think Mercy Curtis is a rival."

"How about just having them come in care of M. Curtis?" Carmichael inquired, wondering how deeply he was going to get involved and what might result.

"Perfect." Mercy glanced around to make sure Mandy wasn't in hearing distance. "Michael, why don't you do something really daring? I read this book where an easterner bought a ranch but didn't know much about running it so he used a different name and then went out and got a job on his own ranch so he could find out all about it."

"Spies and counterspies?" Carmichael grinned. Yet the boldness of the plan appealed to his new, adventuresome nature. Why not? He could meet Desert Rose Birchfield without her knowing his identity, for a while.

FOUR

Dr. Adam Birchfield believed range lore and survival skills as important to his daughters' health as good food and plenty of sleep and exercise. His wife Laurel agreed, as did her twin sister Ivy and her husband, Nathaniel Birchfield, Antelope's beloved minister. These beliefs worked in favor of Desert Rose and Columbine and Nate and Sam who spent all the time they could on their grandparents' ranch, the Double B.

Rose's interest in keeping up with the daring Nate dismayed a score of would-be suitors who often found themselves left to young Columbine's mercies. Even the most devoted and love-stricken cowboy had not touched her heart, although many had won her admiration with his riding, roping, and marksmanship skills.

Yet when a triumphant Nate sought her out waving a letter and whispering, in case Columbine or Sam lurked about, "It's come!" Rose's heart lurched.

"So soon? How did they get it published already?" She snatched the envelope and her eyes opened wide. "Why, this isn't from *Hand and Heart.* It's from Concord, Massachusetts."

"Of course it is." Nate's dark eyes flashed with mirth. "Some eager swain evidently wrote the moment he saw your advertisement. Open it, will you?" The letter from his former teacher had been carefully removed from the larger envelope that came so the one Rose now held could be delivered intact.

Fun filled Rose's expressive face. She ripped open the letter and silently began to read. "Why, he knows you!" she gasped. "Listen to this, Nate. He says there must only be one Nate Birchfield in Antelope. What an odd coincidence."

Nate bent over to twitch a piece of sage off his pants leg and mumbled, "That's probably why he felt it would be safe to write, seeing as we used my address."

"Oh." Rose returned to the letter. "He sounds nice. Is he?"

Nate didn't need to pretend. "He's just plain grand and the only reason I even considered going back for another year." His enthusiasm showed in every word and

Rose listened hard, holding one finger to mark the place in her letter where she stopped reading.

"Carmichael Blake-Jones. What a name!" She threw back her head and laughed until the hills echoed with her joy. "What does he look like?"

"About my height but heavier, fair instead of dark. Better than that, he's willing to see the other man's side of things."

"Is he a Christian?"

Nate cocked his head to one side. "Well," he drawled. "He attended chapel and church. I don't know how deep his faith goes. I know even the most critical of those at school never knew him to do an unkind or unfair thing. Several times for someone in trouble he —"

"Were you one of them?" she demanded, her dark brown eyes glowing.

"Let's just say that even someone as angelic as I slips now and then," he teased then made a halolike motion above his rumpled dark hair.

"Do you think I should answer?" Rose quickly finished the rest of the short letter. "Oh, I know he isn't interested in moving out here or doing any of the things I put in that silly advertisement. He just sounds nice and maybe a bit lonely."

All Nate's mischief fled. "Both his parents were killed in a railway accident a few months ago and he lives in the family home alone except for a housekeeper, Mandy."

"Doesn't he have brothers and sisters?"

"All older and married, busy with their own families. He has a young niece Mercy. I vaguely remember seeing her a time or two."

"Aha!" Rose seized on his statement. "Pretty?"

Nate shrugged. "I guess so. Plumpish, fair. Pretty skin." He surveyed Rose's tanned complexion. "Pink and white, not tanned like yours."

She bristled and he quickly added, "On you it looks good. On her it wouldn't. What else did he say?"

Rose's firm chin shot skyward. "It's my letter, not yours."

"Don't forget I'm your go-between," he warned.

"Not for long." She tucked the letter back into its envelope and shoved it in her shirt pocket. "When I write I'll ask Mr. Blake-Jones to write directly to me from now on."

"How will you explain to your parents the sudden influx of letters in a masculine hand from 2000 miles away?" Nate fired his best shot.

"There won't be a sudden influx," she reminded him. "Besides, I'll tell the truth, well, part of it. I'll tell Mother Mr. Blake-Jones is lonely and you fixed it up for us to correspond."

"Thanks a heap!" He glared at her. "She'll tell my folks and there won't be a doghouse in Wyoming big enough for me."

"Don't be silly," Rose told her irate cousin. "Mother knows what it's like to want to do out-of-the-ordinary things." Her white teeth flashed. "Writing to a perfectly respectable teacher at a private boys' school is a lot different from leaving home and traveling alone to the Wyoming Territory a generation ago!"

Out maneuvered, Nate couldn't help prodding, "When are you going to answer?"

Rose just smiled. "Shame on you, trying to get at the secrets of a maiden's heart."

Nate parried her thrust with a quick retreat, only stopping to call around the corner, "I see you've been reading romances again. Ohhhh, love is soooo grand." He crossed his eyes, stumbled in a mock swoon, then recovered himself and vanished with a mocking laugh.

She couldn't help joining in the laugh. Good old Nate! Suddenly a pang went through her. What if *he* had met a girl back

East he cared enough about to move there himself? *If that ever happened, well, life would hold no surprises for her. He didn't, she told herself. So stop building mountains.*

Her fingers stole to the letter and a warm feeling for the lonely young man who had so courteously answered her advertisement took root in the rich, sympathetic soil of her heart. Perhaps it wasn't proper to reply at once, but who cared? Rose tossed her head and went to find writing materials. . . .

Summer opened in a new and different way from any other. Almost before Rose caught her breath and confessed to her mother that she had actually answered a letter from one of Nate's former teachers, a second letter came. In a way, it offered relief. Rose openly showed it to her parents.

"I wouldn't have chosen this way for you to begin writing to the young man," Dr. Birchfield said. "On the other hand, having a friend from back East can benefit you both and Nate assures me this Mr. Blake-Jones is above reproach." His dark eyes so like Rose's twinkled. "Although Nate isn't always the most reliable judge of character, when it comes down to what really counts I value his comments. Write away, Rose. Just don't encourage your friend to pull up stakes and move to Antelope, at least not until you're eighteen."

"Adam!" Laurel sounded shocked then laughed until her pretty face crinkled and she looked almost as young as her daughters. "I distinctly remember some other easterners pulling up their stakes and look what happened."

"That's what I'm afraid of," he told her solemnly, but Rose saw the twinkle deepen when he kissed her mother.

One evening before sunset Rose saddled Mesquite and rode up to her favorite overlook. She carried with her the latest letter from Massachusetts. New feelings stirred in her heart that thrilled yet frightened her. *Was this what falling in love was like?* To wait impatiently from the time she wrote to Michael, as he had begged her to call him, until a letter came? To seek solitude rather than open the letters in front of curious Columbine and taunting Nate?

With her new awareness, Rose mulled over the changes in herself. "I spend more time dreaming," she admitted to the fiery edge of the sun still visible over the peaks. Color brighter than the blushing sky crept into Rose's cheeks and a wistful sigh escaped. Just this evening after supper she had come upon her father and mother in a rare moment of freedom from their duties. Adam and Laurel had ridden out from town to eat with the Browns and the Birchfield offspring, then had slipped away for a quiet walk. Screened by a drooping cottonwood, Rose stopped short at the picture before her. As Dad faced Mother with their hands joined, their profiles showed clear against the big rock where they stood.

Not wanting to intrude on their precious privacy, Rose took a silent step back then halted, transfixed by Dad's words that fell like beads from a broken string, each separate and ringing.

"Laurel, it's been almost twenty years since I came riding in to Red Cedars. You're more beautiful now than you were then."

The unwilling eavesdropper's eyes stung. Would anyone be able to say that to her twenty or more years from now?

Laurel laughed and little bells rang. "And Dr. Adam Birchfield is even handsomer."

Etched against the moss-covered rock, Adam's face shone with a light that caused Rose to cover her mouth. "Thank God you are the one He knew would complete my life. Dearest, all these years, through drought and hard work, two steps forward and one step back, if you could do it all over, would you leave Red Cedars and come to me again?"

Laurel hesitated and the listening Rose held her breath. Then in a choked voice her mother said, "I would come, only far sooner!"

When Dad caught her close with a little cry, Rose escaped undetected. A knowledge she didn't know she possessed whispered inside her wildly beating heart. *This is love as God meant it to be, enduring, sustaining, real.*

Why should the name Carmichael Blake-Jones immediately flash into her mind? Rose dismissed such premonitions in her usual style. Yet now as the sky changed to gold and purple and gray and she reluctantly mounted Mesquite for the ride home, memory of the two who were dearer to Rose than anyone on earth settled into her heart's treasure chest to be stored, taken out now and then, and cherished.

News that ran the range like wildfire temporarily replaced thoughts of love from Rose's mind. When Nate rode in from Antelope with another letter from Michael he also delivered the news that Old Man Turpin had sold his Circle 5 ranch to an easterner.

"Wish I'd known," said Thomas Brown, scratching his head as he looked at his grandson. "We might have swung it and added to the Double B."

Grandma Sadie, bright and perky as ever, said, "Land sakes, old man, don't you think we have enough to do around here without adding another ranch?"

Thomas grinned and Rose saw the fondness in the gaze he turned toward his wife. "The young people are growing up. Maybe one of them will want a ranch."

Nate squirmed under his grandfather's direct gaze. He still hadn't told anyone except Rose about his struggle over the future. His younger brother Sam grinned back at Grandpa Thomas. "Not me. I'm gonna be a doctor like Uncle Adam." With a flash of the mischief that characterized Nate, young Sam drawled, "Too bad you didn't buy it for Rose. She could be a female rancher. She'd do a good job too," he added.

"You just bet I would. If I had the Circle 5 I'd tear down those saggy fences and build a strong corral and then build a house with enough windows to see all five peaks that show up there."

"Does anyone know anything about the new owner?" Columbine put in. Her light brown hair lay in carefully set curls and her usually languid brown eyes sparkled with excitement. "Does he have a family? Will he be living on the Circle 5?"

"Uh, Old Man Turpin says everything was handled through what he calls 'a young upstart of a Rock Springs lawyer.' The name on the papers is a Mr. Prentice." Nate meticulously refrained from mentioning one small detail: He had encouraged the new owner to use a name other than Blake-Jones. Michael had chosen his mother's maiden name and in correspondence had frankly told the lawyer he preferred the countryside didn't know his real identity until a later time when he would disclose it. Neither did Nate report how the lawyer verbally raised his eyebrows but buttoned his lip in respect to his eccentric client's wishes.

"The lawyer is rounding up hands, doing some of those repairs you talked about, Rosy, and in general, sprucing up the Circle 5." Repressed excitement oozed from Nate.

Rose glanced at him sharply. "You act as if you struck the entire deal."

Nate grinned his particularly maddening grin. "Well, I did bring home the news, didn't I?" He tweaked her braid. "Ready for a ride?"

"Five minutes." She raced upstairs to get a jacket and the sombrero she liked best for riding.

Trail companions Mesquite and Piebald

stood waiting by the time she arrived. She'd had some trouble convincing Columbine and Sam this wasn't a good time for them to come along.

"Come on, Columbine, I'll take you," she heard Sam say and some of her guilt fled. She had to tell Nate a piece of news of her own. In the letter she'd managed to slip away and read, Michael shared that after a long time of serious thought he had decided to take time off from his teaching position and do some traveling.

Don't stop writing, he wrote in the concise hand Rose had come to admire. *Send letters in care of M. Curtis and they will be forwarded.*

"M. Curtis?" Nate wrinkled his forehead. "Who's that?"

"Who cares?" Rose said impatiently and swung to the saddle. Her auburn braid flipped over one shoulder, she felt Mesquite stamp his hoof, ready for the ride. "What if Michael — Mr. Jones comes out here?"

Nate had never looked more innocent. "What if he does? I told you he's a grand guy." He vaulted onto Piebald and gathered the reins. Not until their usual race ended with him a length ahead did Nate casually add, "Don't you want him to come?"

"I don't know." Panting, her face as pink as her name, Rose slowly dismounted and dropped to the needle-covered knoll they loved. "He hasn't sent a picture, although I did when he asked for one."

Nate choked and she whirled on him. "What's wrong with you?"

He coughed. "Then you wouldn't know him if he came riding up to you." He jerked off his big hat and slapped dust from his jeans with it until Rose indignantly moved away from him. "Any other reason you aren't pitty-patting to see him?"

She ignored his sarcasm and drank in the familiar scene before her. Gazing at the rolling hills and tall mountains, she was filled with the strength and peace of the Psalmist David: "I will lift up mine eyes unto the hills, from whence cometh my help."*

"Nate —" A childish tremble brought seriousness to her cousin's face. "It's been wonderful to write and tell him about Wyoming and hear about his life. Sometimes, though, when you meet someone about whom you have certain ideas, you feel disappointed."

"I know, Rose Red."

The hated nickname slipped by without a murmur. "I just don't want anything to spoil the way things are right now." She opened

*Psalm 121:1 (KJV).

69

her arms wide to the panorama before them.

Nate stayed quiet so long she looked at him in surprise. He lay on his stomach chewing a blade of grass. The expression in his eyes touched his faithful friend's heart. "Here I am worrying about what may never happen while you're struggling. Are you any closer to an answer?"

"I think so." New manliness shone in the dark gaze he tore from the mountains and turned on her. "Nothing shattering has happened, but every time I see Dad's tired face filled with a look beyond explaining I see myself." He shifted. "Does that sound stupid?"

Rose shook her head. "Have you talked with him or Aunt Ivy?"

"I won't until I'm sure." Nate moodily returned to his surveyal of the valley below. "If it were any other job I'd probably be shouting it from the housetops. Like Sam's hung on your dad's pants leg from babyhood talking about being a doctor."

"I understand, Nate." Rose put her sturdy, tanned hand over her cousin's and love flowed between them.

"You're a good kid, Rosy." Nate turned his hand over, gripped hers, and sat up. "Sometimes I think we're almost twins." The next moment he flung off such sentiment and reverted to his usual self. "Why don't we ride over to the Circle 5 tomorrow?" Only the look in his eyes betrayed how important these few moments had been to him.

"Why don't we take Columbine and Sam?" she suggested and sprang lightly to her feet. "Seems we've spent most of our lives running away from them. Lately Columbine has acted lonely."

"Let's fill our saddlebags with grub so we can take all the time we want." Nate leaped at the idea. "Can't go in the morning, though. Grandpa needs help mending fences or they'll start looking like those tumbledown ones on the Circle 5."

"Never!" She laughed. "Besides, this Mr. Prentice is going to fix them, you said."

A curious light came into Nate's eyes. "He's a real good fixer, according to Old Man Turpin's lawyer."

That night the entire household including the four young Birchfields turned in early. Usually the cousins quietly visited for a time after Thomas and Sadie went to bed. Tonight they wanted all the sleep they could get and planned to arise even earlier than normal so work could be done and they'd have time for their ride.

Rose could scarcely believe how excited

Columbine was over getting to go. She observed her younger sister pulling on boots and retying her scarf for the third time. "How tall are you now?" she asked.

"Still just five foot three." Columbine's fair skin flushed. "I look taller in boots, though, don't I?"

"You really do." Softened by her own thoughts of romance and growing up, Rose curbed her impatience at Columbine and gave her sister a hug. "You may be short but you're a lot more grown up than you used to be."

"So are you," Columbine told her. She glanced down and her dark lashes made little half-moons on her pink cheeks. "Ever since you started getting letters from Nate's friend and teacher you've been, well, nicer." She looked up and Rose saw sincerity in the brown eyes.

At that, Rose swiftly looked in the mirror. Had she really changed? Her image denied it: same auburn hair in a fat braid with the end curling, same dark brown eyes. Or were they really the same?

Rose shivered but quickly hid it from her observant sister by shrugging her shoulders under her worn riding shirt. Her little pretense did not fool Columbine.

"We all change, Rose. Remember when

Paul said he put childish things away when he became a man?"* She set her sombrero on her brown curls and finished, "I'll be sixteen in mid-September. You'll be eighteen less than two months later. Many girls our age are married and some have babies." Her face glowed. "Who knows when God will send a special someone like Dad or Uncle Nathaniel, or even like Nate?" Laughter bubbled from her and died. "We have to be ready."

What if God already had sent someone, a teacher named Michael? Rose crushed the thought but a rich blush caught her unaware.

★1 Corinthians 13:11 (KJV)

FIVE

Alone with his thoughts and unable to sleep, Nate Birchfield had at last fled the Double B into the starry Wyoming night. In the distance faint snatches of song could be heard, most likely night riders checking their herds. Several neighboring ranchers had reported missing cattle recently and rumors that a new and daring rustler band had moved into the area were adrift. Increased efforts to protect the animals were in place because as one wise rancher put it, "The way I see it, if a man steals our cattle he strips the food off our tables."

Tonight, however, Nate's mind could not be troubled with livestock. The smell of sage and wildflowers, the crooning of the night wind, and soft neighing from the corral called him. Fifteen minutes later Piebald and his rider quietly walked away from the Double B and broke into a trot, then a canter, and at last a full gallop. Nate knew the dangers of galloping a horse at night — gopher holes and unexpected shadows that made a horse nervous — so he kept to the well-traveled road to Antelope. Long before reaching its outskirts, he slowed Piebald and turned toward a patch where the faithful horse could graze.

Rose's question haunted him. Although Nate had determined to have the summer free, he hadn't been able to outride or outrun God. More and more he felt the challenge of the ministry.

"Never could understand how folks could think a preacher's a weakling," he mumbled to the swaying evergreen branches. "Seems to me if a fellow's going to work for God, it will take everything he's got." He found a fallen limb and dug the end of it into the ground. A great lump came to his throat. How many times had he seen his father down the town's worst men with courage and flashing dark eyes? A view from a crack in a building or a partly drawn shade showed much. Nate had watched Antelope's minister comfort the dying, tell the story of Jesus to a scantily clad woman dying from a careless gunshot in the saloon where she worked, and pray with parents whose only child died of fever.

If he lived to be older than Methuselah

Nate wouldn't forget that last scene. He had sneaked out of the house the way he often did when his father was called in the night, following at a discreet distance. He never knew what compelled him to go, perhaps fear for his father's safety or the desire to be on hand in case Nat needed him.

That night he shivered in the cold outside the crude log home that held tragedy, and more, and listened.

"Don't talk to me about God," bellowed the young father who always smiled at Nate and Sam. "What does God know about how I feel? Why didn't He make my boy get well? He's my only son, you hear me? God didn't spare my only son!"

Nate stood awed at the grief, forgetting how cold he was, waiting for his father's answer. When it came, it nearly rocked the young boy out of his shoes.

"God knows exactly how you feel." No mumbled apology or stumbling comfort but truth, raw and searing. "God lost His only son too. He could have spared Jesus but He didn't. He watched the very people He loved enough to send that only Son hang Him up on a cross and spit on Him. Oh yes, God knows what it is like to lose an only Son and because He has gone through it, He can and will help you, if you let Him."

A loud cry mingled with the softer weeping of the bereaved mother. "It's all right, Steve," Nathaniel continued. "God understands your pain and anger. He knows it's like the poison my brother Adam has to get out of festered wounds before they heal. Don't be ashamed. Right this minute God is probably weeping right along with you."

Nate vanished into the night. He never told his father what he heard but neither did he forget it. Now on a far different kind of night years later, Nate wondered. *Had his soul been touched that moment that seemed like days ago? Had God placed it into his heart to trail his beloved father for this purpose?*

The peaceful night offered no answers; God would choose the time and place for further revelation. Nate led Piebald back to the road, mounted, and again built up to a full gallop, his hair streaming back and his face aglow. Perhaps he imagined it, but when he silently prayed for answers the wind seemed to respond *sooon, sooon,* and home at last he tumbled back into bed content to wait.

Nate didn't awaken until Sam's eager hand shook him with the reminder that fences waited and so did the girls.

A collective gasp went up from the cousins

when they reined in on the crest of a hill that gave them a view of the Circle 5.

"It looks like an anthill I saw after I accidentally stepped on it," Sam told them.

Rose glued her gaze on the multitude of men working below her. "Mercy, how did Mr. Prentice get so many so fast?" she gasped, almost unable to believe her own vision. "Why, they've already torn down the old corral and refenced. Look!" She pointed to the barn. "It's been shored up."

"And it's getting a new roof," Nate said with obvious satisfaction.

"They aren't doing anything to the house," Columbine complained. She patted her horse with pretty, gloved fingers and giggled. "There can't be a Mrs. Prentice or she'd insist that the house be repaired first!"

"I wouldn't," Rose cried indignantly. "If new stock is coming in, especially horses, the corral and barn are more important. Once they're done, there's plenty of time before winter to fix the house."

"I can just see Mr. Prentice," Columbine retorted. "He's probably a paunchy, middle-aged retired banker who reads western stories. He won't take kindly to sleeping in a house with a leaky roof."

"How do you know it leaks?" Rose demanded, her cheeks on fire. "It looks all right to me." She glanced at the shabby cabin. "Besides, your paunchy, middle-aged retired banker will be a whole lot healthier if he will throw down some blankets under one of those big pine trees and roll up in them for a few nights."

Nate had a sudden coughing spell that left him red-faced and panting. He finally croaked, "Let's ride down and see what the workers have to say."

The clatter of hooves announced the visitors' arrival even above pounding hammers and chewing saws. First to notice and greet them was a blond-haired, amber-eyed man who appeared to be in his early forties. At perhaps five feet nine inches he looked taller because of his high-heeled boots. Rose wondered why his eyes narrowed almost to slits when he looked first at her, then at Columbine.

"Welcome to the Circle 5." He doffed a new-looking sombrero and stooped gracefully into a low bow. "You are — ?"

"Nate and Sam Birchfield and our cousins Desert Rose and Columbine." Nate swung out of the saddle and held out his hand. "Are you the new foreman?"

"You might say that." He laughed carelessly. "Won't you step down? I'm Daniel Sharpe, glad to meet you."

A little bell rang deep in Rose's mind. She looked at Nate, whose puzzled face reflected her own uncertainty. Surely she had heard the name before in a way that made her glad Nate was there.

"You're really fixing the old place up, I see." Sam broke the awkward silence. In the moments that had passed a look from Nate told Rose Nate had remembered Daniel Sharpe. A spate of explanations by the new Circle 5 foreman ended when Nate interrupted at the first possible moment.

"Sorry to rush off." The words rolled out easily but Nate herded his little band back to their horses. "We have quite a ways to ride."

"Of course you do," Dan Sharpe agreed amiably. Yet Rose felt the sarcastic flick of his look toward her with its hint of boldness.

"Goodbye, Mr. Sharpe." Columbine never let an opportunity pass to practice her innocent wiles. "Do come and visit us. We're staying at the Double B and —" A sharp jab in her ribs brought a look of astonishment toward her sister but effectively ended the farewell. "Why did you do that?" Columbine demanded the moment they were out of earshot.

"Don't tell the story of your life to every

stranger you meet," Rose snapped.

"Why not? He seemed nice and he's going to be our neighbor and —"

"Some neighbor!" Nate exploded. "Don't you know who Dan Sharpe is?"

"The new foreman of the Circle 5," Sam put in and laughed. It faded into the mountain air when Nate glared at him.

"Who *is* Daniel or Dan Sharpe?" Rose asked. "The name sounds familiar but I can't remember where I've heard it."

"I didn't either, at first." Nate's lips set in a white line. "Then it hit me. He's the crook who robbed the Rock Springs bank almost twenty years ago."

"That nice man?" Columbine's brown eyes looked disbelieving.

Nate spit out his words. "That nice man also kidnapped Aunt Laurel and held her in a lonely mountain cabin, along with my mother who trailed them! If Dad and Uncle Adam hadn't gotten Running Deer to track them, who knows what might have happened!"

"I remember now that Dad said a man named Dan Sharpe went to prison for robbing a bank but I never heard the rest of the story," Rose cried. "How could anyone be so wicked?"

"I guess he fell for Aunt Laurel then Mom

when they first came out here," Nate continued. "You probably wouldn't have heard the rest of the story so keep your mouths shut. It's coming back now. You know when I was a little kid how I used to hide under the couch and listen to everything?"

"Last year?" Rose inquired sweetly.

He ignored her. "Well, what happened was that Dan got hurt at the cabin and after Aunt Laurel and Mom found the bank loot they got him tied up. They knew if Antelope found out Dan had held them prisoner some of the men would hang him. They couldn't stand that so they made a deal that Dan would admit the robbery but they swore not to tell about the kidnapping. I remember Aunt Laurel saying she was so glad they had because otherwise they would always have been filled with hate and Christians aren't supposed to hate people. Mom and Aunt Laurel never told anyone."

"My stars, how romantic!" Columbine breathed. "Just imagine, getting kidnapped and carried off then forgiving the perpetrator of the dark deed!"

Rose's new sympathy for her sister died with what had to be a direct quote from one of Columbine's syrupy novels. "Don't be ridiculous."

Columbine's eyes opened wide. "I think

the poor man shows in his eyes how much he's suffered." She gave Sam a dark look when he snorted. "Well, he does. All that time in prison. They must have let him go for good behavior."

"Or because his sentence was up," Nate put in. "If you have any idea of seeing Dan Sharpe, Columbine, forget it right now."

She tossed her head. "I still feel sorry for him. Wouldn't it be beautiful if he came back to show everyone he had repented? We're told to love our enemies, aren't we?" She giggled. "Since we don't have any real enemies, does he count?"

"You won't be seeing anything of him," Rose told her. "He wouldn't have the nerve to face Mother and Aunt Ivy." She touched her heels to her horse, eager to put miles between her and the man whose amber eyes had glowed like a mountain lion's.

Rose's evaluation proved to be false. On the next Sunday afternoon Dan Sharpe rode in to the Double B and hitched his shining buckskin horse to the rail as if he worked there.

The usual Sunday afternoon gathering of family and friends lounged on the wide porch. Hardwick, the grizzled owner of the nearby Lazy H, sat tilted back in a chair. When the visitor appeared, the chair crashed to the porch floor and the sturdy man leaped to his feet. "By the powers, is it — it can't be Dan Sharpe?"

In the frozen silence that seemed to chill the warm afternoon, Dan Sharpe slid from his saddle with pantherlike grace. "Howdy, folks." He pushed his spotless Stetson to the back of his shining head and removed it in one easy motion. "Glad to see so many of you congregated here."

Rose quickly glanced at Nate, who shook his head in warning. Sam and Columbine stared open-mouthed, but Rose didn't trust the look in her pretty sister's face.

"Sharpe." Thomas Brown offered a noncommittal greeting then slowly got up but Rose noticed he didn't offer his hand. Neither did anyone else.

Dan's gaze traveled from Nathaniel and Adam Birchfield to their wives, Ivy Ann and Laurel. A sardonic smile vanished so quickly Rose wondered if it had really been there. "I just wanted to come tell you all that I had a lot of time to think these past years in my, er, accommodations. This is by way of an apology for the wrong trails I rode in the past." Dan's frankness of speech and manner brought surprised gasps from his listeners.

He's enjoying playing the prodigal son. Rose

could almost hear the words. *I don't think he's sorry at all. For some reason it's necessary to him to put on this humility.*

Columbine's I-told-you-so smirk and the fatuous smile she bestowed on the penitent man left Rose trembling with rage. Couldn't she see through Dan Sharpe, standing there hat in hand?

To Rose's amazement, Uncle Nat crossed the porch and held out his hand in welcome. "This is good news for all of us, Dan."

Rose thought she would explode when the self-invited guest had the audacity to murmur, "The influence of the two Mrs. Birchfields long ago is what made me realize how much I'd left my early teachings."

"So what are you doing back in these parts?" Hardwick squinted and Rose had the feeling he was no more convinced of Sharpe's sincerity than she.

"When I no longer needed my former accommodations I looked around for a job." Innocence and gratitude didn't quite erase the preying look from Dan's amber eyes. "The word got out about the Circle 5 being sold. I went straight to the Rock Springs lawyer who is handling the sale and threw myself on his mercy."

Rose felt laughter bubble inside her when she compared the literary tastes of Dan and

Columbine. *Threw myself on his mercy* faithfully appeared and reappeared in Columbine's stories, at least the few Rose had been able to wade through.

"So you're getting another chance." Nate's voice sounded hoarse but deceptively bland. One dark eyebrow raised slightly, a sure signal to Rose how her cousin felt.

"I think it's wonderful, Mr. Sharpe," Columbine gushed. Her carefully nurtured complexion blended perfectly with the rosy gown she wore.

"Thank you, Miss Columbine." Dan turned Rose's way. "Well, Miss Birchfield, aren't you going to welcome your new neighbor?" Little devils seemed to dance in his strange eyes.

"Welcome, Mr. Sharpe," Rose obediently repeated then lightly jumped to her feet. "Here, take my chair. Nate and I are going to fix cold lemonade. It's such a warm afternoon." Her plain white dress that she wore under protest on Sundays fluttered about her.

"May I help?"

"Oh, no thank you. Nate is the only one I need." Let him find the hidden meaning in that if he can and get the look from his eyes that she detested. Admiration from the range riders always carried respect. The measuring examination of her by Dan Sharpe did not.

Before she and Nate stepped inside Rose heard Dan begin another verse of how sorry he was and that he planned to make the Circle 5 a paying proposition.

"For himself, not for the new owner, I bet." Nate attacked the lemons as though he had Sharpe in his two strong hands. A worried look showed his concern for that new owner. "Mr. Prentice may find himself broke and ruined if my instincts are true."

"I can't understand why Uncle Nat treated him so warmly." Rose took glasses from the cupboard and put them on a tray.

"Dad feels there's a spark of God in every person and we must always try to fan that spark until it grows into a fire that purifies even the blackest heart," Nate told her.

"Columbine certainly seems to agree," Rose said bitterly. "Just listen." She and Nate leaned closer to the screened kitchen window, open to capture what little breeze there was. Dan Sharpe had shifted his chair closer to the girl and his bent head showed rapt attention.

"It's truly an inspiration for someone who has been bad, well, mistaken, to admit it and go on from there." Columbine's high, clear voice made Rose feel sick.

"We'll stop that in a hurry." Nate finished squeezing the lemons as if his life depended on it, dumped in sugar and cold water, and vigorously stirred the pitcherful until Rose warned him it would break from the onslaught. A few minutes later Nate marched back out to the porch followed by Rose with the glasses. "Come and get it, folks." He glanced at Columbine. "Say, are any of those delicious cookies left you baked yesterday?"

"Of course."

"Would you mind getting them, Columbine? Rose and I will pour and pass."

His strategy worked. Dan Sharpe courteously stood until Rose finished passing the glasses and although she hated it, Rose settled into Columbine's chair. Nate finished pouring the lemonade and dropped to the chair on Dan's other side.

"Is the new Circle 5 owner planning to take possession soon?" Nate queried innocently.

Dan's careless laugh sent dismay playing up and down Rose's spine. "I doubt it. He's an eastern dude who won't know anything about handling cattle and horses and riders. I'll be in full control, so he won't have anything to worry about."

Oh, won't he? Rose wanted to yell. *If you*

were in full control of the Double B I'd be worried sick. She bit her lip. Now was *not* the time to show animosity, with Columbine crowded close beside her obviously drinking in every word Dan Sharpe uttered.

Somehow they got through the hideous afternoon. Rose talked and laughed and rejoiced when Sharpe's attention turned more and more to her, with Columbine, Nate, and Sam background figures. Suppose she could win this man's confidence and learn why he had really come back. Or would her playing with fire result in an unknown blaze she wouldn't be able to stop? Undecided, she unconsciously heaved a great sigh of relief when all the company left, Dan Sharpe last of all.

That night Nate Birchfield wrote an urgent, troubled letter to Carmichael Blake-Jones, care of M. Curtis, with an underlined request that the letter be forwarded immediately.

SIX

Carmichael Blake-Jones had always hated his long name, a name made even longer with "Carey" as a middle name. "Carmichael Carey Blake-Jones," he often scoffed. "It's probably as long as I was when I came into this world." Now, for the first time, it came in handy: He could choose bits and pieces for his nom de plume. At Mercy's urging, Michael intended to arrive in Antelope and, if possible, find work on the Circle 5 under the short and simple alias Mike Carey. Nondescript enough to pass in the West yet simple and familiar to Michael, the name was unlikely to trip him up when someone addressed him that way.

When all the legal papers that gave him ownership of the Circle 5 arrived, he laughed at himself. Who would purchase an unseen ranch in an unknown state on the word of a former student? His doubts were somewhat subdued when he remembered the integrity of Nate Birchfield, evidenced in all their former dealings.

When Carmichael Carey Blake-Jones, alias Mr. Prentice, alias Mike Carey, swung aboard the train muttering Horace Greeley's famous piece of advice, "Go West, young man," he was still filled with a kind of awe at his own daring. If a self-styled prophet had told him a few months ago he'd be cutting ties with everything he knew and setting forth in search of adventure, Michael would have laughed. Now Mike Carey merely smiled. A few turns of the great wheels and he'd be around the first bend.

"Don't forget everything we discussed," Mercy called from her position trackside. Mischief curled her lips upward and Michael saw the despairing what-on-earth-now look his sister Caroline gave her husband.

"I won't." He waved until Mercy's dainty lace handkerchief became a small white spot then vanished when the train gathered speed.

The same journey that had thrilled the Birchfields and Browns years before severed the young teacher from his past and effectively changed Michael into Mike Carey. At Mercy's instigation he had selected rough clothing to fit his new station in life and she had insisted on washing it a few times so it no longer looked new. She had also insisted that he deliberately scuff the new boots so their shine wouldn't betray him.

A dozen times Michael laughed at the determined girl but secretly marveled at how knowledgeable she had grown concerning Wyoming. "Clothes may look worn but how am I going to conceal the fact I am a tenderfoot?" he demanded.

Mercy even had an answer for that. Her round face dimpled. "Easy. You don't go straight to Antelope. You stop off before you get there, stay a few days, find a deserted cabin or someplace where you won't be bothered, then practice roping and shooting all by yourself."

"You think I can learn all that in a few days?" He shook his head in disbelief. "And all this time I thought you were smart for your age."

She refused to be baited. "You already ride, except you'll have to get used to a western saddle. I'll bet you find out the rest isn't as hard as you expect it will be."

Now, with every *clackety-clack* of the wheels carrying him closer to the ranch he couldn't even begin to know how to run Mike wondered. He found himself turning to God, as he had tentatively begun to do throughout the summer. Long talks with Mercy, who loved the Lord and didn't hesitate to condemn her uncle for the bitterness he confessed, had rekindled in his heart the desire for the companionship with God he once treasured. The many hours on the train gave him time to remember all the things Mercy and he talked about at the end of the day.

Two weeks later Mike felt ready to plunge into the world of the Circle 5. He had followed Mercy's advice to the letter, found an out-of-the-way spot and shot up trees, fence posts, and a multitude of tin cans. Once he had been caught out overnight when he inexpertly tied his rented horse and shivered under a tree until a compassionate moon shed its light and he could see the way back to his shack. Mike Carey learned that night why cowboys and ranchers hated walking and cherished even the poorest excuse of a horse. The boot heels so needed for riding had not been designed for a man afoot.

Every time Mike hit his target, he whooped. At the end of such active days he discovered how good even the simple meals he could manage tasted. Not that he didn't miss Mandy's cooking! A dozen times he told prairie dogs and chipmunks, "I just have to get her out here." Their interested expressions made him laugh.

At first, Mike hadn't wanted anyone in Wyoming to know who he was. After much reflection he changed his mind. The time might come when he would need the backing of someone respected and trusted. His Rock Springs lawyer — recommended by Nate as the "only guy around if you want an honest lawyer" — fit the description. The afternoon before Mike planned to head for Antelope, he sought out the attorney, introduced himself, and disclosed his plan to get work on his own ranch. The lawyer's "You may just get by with it" meant more to Mike than anything he could have said.

The beauty of the Wind River Range topped anything Mike had ever seen. In the moment he first glimpsed the peaks and valleys, silver streams and forests, grazing land, and piercing blue sky, he turned traitor to the stormy Atlantic he had loved. He had all he could do to keep from racing the strong and spirited quarter horse he had purchased in Rock Springs on the advice of his lawyer. "His name's Peso and it fits him," the attorney said. "He came to me in partial payment of a bad debt. I don't have need of a cutting horse but you will."

Mike stroked the horse's powerful, reddish-brown neck. "Why is he named Peso?"

"A peso is a Mexican dollar and a good quarter horse can pivot on a spot just about that small." A wintry smile lightened the attorney's eyes. "In case you're wondering, a cutting horse does just that, cuts or sorts out cattle from a herd."

"Thanks." Mike grinned at his own ignorance. "Think I'll ever learn what I need to know to run the Circle 5?"

"I wouldn't be a bit surprised. Besides, your foreman knows ranching and cattle. I hesitated when Dan Sharpe came to me because he spent some years in prison for robbing the bank here in Rock Springs, but —"

Mike felt like Peso had kicked him in the stomach. "You mean my foreman is a bank robber?"

"Former bank robber," his lawyer reminded him. "Out here we tend to give folks second chances if they are worth it."

"And Dan Sharpe is worth it?"

"He appears to be sincere. As the graybeards say, truth will win out." The wintry smile reappeared. "Just keep your eyes wide open and don't be afraid to contact me if you need to."

Mike raised one eyebrow in the way that made his face look more innocent than ever. "Is there anything I need to know about the rest of my employees, uh, ranch hands?"

The attorney's rare laugh rang out and he unexpectedly dropped a heavy hand to Mike's shoulder. "Just that they're a bunch of rowdy, lovable, ornery, soul-trying boys, some still in their teens. They will play tricks, wait to see how you take them, drive you crazy, and, once you pass their tests, settle down into a loyal crew who will stand behind you in high water . . . and its companion."

Sobered, dreading those tests yet determined not to fail, Mike gripped the other's hand, then swung into the saddle. He caught the approval in his lawyer's eyes and secretly rejoiced over the hours he had spent riding back home. At least he didn't have to learn that, along with everything else!

"Now, you can't help your accent," his new mentor told him. "I'd recommend listening a whole lot more than you talk. You'll learn more that way too," he said cryptically. "Good luck, you'll need it. One more thing: Never lend that horse to anyone."

Mike turned Peso north, the advice ringing in his ears. "Well, Peso, looks like strange pastures ahead. Wonder why he said never to lend you to anyone? I hated to show any more ignorance than I had to. Maybe it's the custom of the country or something."

Peso's steady *clip-clop* covered miles of road, steadily winding upward bringing them closer to Antelope. Once Mike reached Antelope there would be little time for riding. To be more authentic, he had left most of his money with his Rock Springs lawyer. "Two reasons," he told Peso, whose soft nicker and toss of head encouraged confidences. "First, if I show up with money folks are bound to be suspicious. Second, if I don't have money I'll have to get a job right away." Mike couldn't decide if his intelligent steed's snort showed agreement or disdain for his new owner.

Years before when Adam Birchfield stood on the crest of a hill and observed Antelope for the first time, he thrilled to the scene. Later, Laurel and her family did the same. History repeated itself when Peso scrambled up a steep place and Mike Carey gazed down into the valley. Early evening shadows and swaying branches softened the rawness of the still-frontierlike town with a purple haze. Only the dim strains of tinkling pianos from the Pronghorn and Silver saloons at either end of town drifted up. A deceptive peace radiated from the town caught between the supper hour and the inevitable promenade later in the evening. Mike slowly rode down the winding road. Every smell, sight, and sound became meaningful.

Armed with Nate's detailed instructions and a letter of introduction from the Rock Springs lawyer, Mike passed through Antelope's business center. The dry goods store, the general store with a surprisingly clean window and attractively arranged display of canned goods, other food and merchandise, and a harness and blacksmith shop all seemed familiar to him because of Nate's crude drawings. Mike finally turned and came to a log church topped with a spire so like the ones in New England that a flash of homesickness touched him. He eagerly looked at the low, log parsonage Nate had described and felt a deep sense of guilt. Could he deceive Nate's wonderful minister father and charming mother? Perhaps he should bypass the welcome he knew Nat and Ivy Ann Birchfield would offer to keep from blundering and giving the whole thing away.

He retraced his way to a large building on a side street with a neat sign outside that read "ROOMS." Better not to chance exposing his identity at the Birchfields. Besides, Nate had said he spent most of the summer out at his grandparents' ranch. After a good night's sleep Mike would decide what to do next.

It didn't take long to arrange for Peso's care at the livery stable and get a room. "Just one night?" the proprietor asked. He didn't seem overly curious, just friendly.

"I hope so." Mike's open manner served him well. "I heard in Rock Springs I might be able to get work up here."

"What can you do?" The man acted more interested.

"Ride, shoot, rope, some of each."

"If you don't mind working for an ex-convict, Dan Sharpe's lookin' for riders." The proprietor eyed Mike keenly.

"What kind of man is he?" Mike parried and tried to hide the exultant leap of his heart.

"We're all waitin' to find that out ourselves." The big man laughed. "Used to be Dan Sharpe was as popular around here as the next one. Antelope's willin' to give him another chance."

"Antelope sounds like a mighty fine little town," Mike said. He signed *Mike Carey* on the register and his landlord peered at the name.

"I used to know some Careys up Montana way. Any kin?"

Mike's spirits plummeted. "No, I'm from parts east of here," he said vaguely. "How much for the night and is there a place I can get something to eat this late?"

The proprietor named a sum so small Mike almost gave himself away laughing, especially when the big man added, "Reckon Mother can find you some supper if you ain't partic'lar."

"I'm not." Mike breathed easier.

An hour later, filled to the bursting point with the first good meal he'd had since he left Mandy, Mike strolled around the little town. He avoided the Pronghorn and the Silver but instead familiarized himself with the different stores and said howdy to a few loungers. He almost came apart when he overheard one of them whisper in a voice loud enough to be heard in Rock Springs, "Who is that feller? S'pose he's lookin' for somebody?"

Mike beat a hasty retreat and laughed all the way back to his spare but spotlessly clean room on the top floor of the rooming-house. Mercy would squeal when she heard her uncle had been mistaken for a gunfighter!

He slept deeply and dreamlessly and

awakened to a rosy dawn. A chill was in the air in spite of the promise of another gorgeous and warm day. *Must be the altitude,* Mike thought. Right after breakfast where he briefly met the few other inhabitants of the roominghouse, Mike headed for the livery stable. Peso stood munching oats and lifting one foot as if impatient to be gone.

"Thanks," Mike told the hostler. "By the way, how do I get to the Circle 5 from here?"

"Thataway." The leathery faced man pointed but shook his head. "You sure you want to ride out there on this horse?"

"Why not?" Astonished, Mike stopped with his hand on the reins.

The hostler cackled. "That's a mighty fine horse, he is. An' Dan Sharpe just natur'ly takes to fine horses."

"Not Peso." Mike laughed and mounted. "I don't sell my friend here."

"I don't remember sayin' anythin' about *sellin'* the horse." The hostler's warning floated after Mike but he just waved and didn't answer. His lawyer's advice came back, *Listen more than you talk . . . you'll learn more.* It had already paid off.

Mike had thought his cup of delight filled when he first saw the Rockies and the Wind River Range. Those moments paled into nothingness when he rode through flower-blessed meadows, up long slopes, and across streams and reined in on the same little knoll above the Circle 5 that the Birchfield cousins had mounted days before.

In involuntary tribute to his Creator, Mike swept his hat off and bowed his head. Could any spot on earth be closer to a little bit of heaven? The five beautiful peaks visible from where he sat dwarfed his very soul. No wonder the original owner, whoever it had been, named the ranch the Circle 5. "Dear God, I could be happy here the rest of my life," Mike whispered from behind the swelling in his breast.

The next moment he jerked as if stung by a bee. The vivacious face of Desert Rose Birchfield that Mike had memorized from her photograph flitted into his mind, completing the picture of years ahead. He saw her kneeling beside him with her tanned hand in his as they dedicated their lives and home to their Master; he saw her thick braid flying above her horse Mesquite, her face laughing yet serious.

Peso raised his head and neighed.

"None too soon," Mike chastised himself. But a dull red glowed in his face and he took a shaky breath to steady himself before making his approach to the Circle 5.

To his amazement, Dan Sharpe little resembled the hardened criminal Mike had imagined. His genuine welcome contrasted with the curious looks from the busy hands. "Say, stranger, are you looking for work?"

"I sure am." Mike dismounted and noticed the admiration in Sharpe's face.

"Good horse there. You didn't steal him, did you?" Underneath the foreman's banter lay something sinister.

"Haw, haw," echoed from the surrounding riders and put Mike on his mettle. He gave his most disarming grin.

"Seems like it was the other way around," he declared. "I never did such horse-trading in my entire life!" He chuckled at the true statement that merely failed to include it was the *only* horse-trading he'd ever done.

"What can you do?" Sharpe demanded, a wary look in his catlike eyes. "Besides ride. I can see that."

"Rope some, shoot some." Mike had the feeling Sharpe's slouch hid a wild beast ready to pounce at the slightest provocation.

"Are you being modest or can you shoot?" one of the hands called.

Before he replied, Mike caught the significance of the question. Obviously the Circle 5 men were more interested in his skills with a gun than with a rope. Could he pass their first test and begin to win the respect he must have to also inspire their loyalty?

"Toss something," he told the riders. His searching gaze discovered a tin can off to one side. "Throw that." While one of the hands reached to get it, Mike silently shot a prayer into the blue Wyoming heavens. *Please, dear God, help me to do my best.*

The can flashed silver in the sunlight. *Spang!* Mike's first shot caught it in the air and sent it flying. The noise drowned Mike's surprised gasp. He hadn't been able to practice on moving objects in his sojourn before reaching Antelope. Thankfulness filled him and left him a bit lightheaded.

"Why didn't you shoot again?" Sharpe's amber gaze bored into Mike. He uncoiled from his relaxed position.

"Why waste bullets when one shot does it?" Mike calmly returned although he wanted to howl along with the hands who evidently liked his humor.

"I guess he can shoot — some," one offered drily.

"Do I get the job?" Mike prodded.

"Yeah. Who are you, anyway? On the dodge?" Sharpe couldn't leave off worrying the bone of contention Mike's shot created.

"Mike Carey." He ignored the second

question. "Where do I bunk?" He bit his lip, glad for the few western words Mercy had taught him.

"You sound like an easterner," Sharpe said disparagingly.

Mike's shoulder muscles tensed. If he took that kind of talk even from his new boss he'd lose the ground gained with the shot. "You have something against easterners?" His innocent, round face must have reassured Sharpe for the foreman immediately shook his head.

"Naw. Some eastern guy named Prentice bought the Circle 5 and he's got the cash to make it a paying ranch." A little smile that didn't reach Sharpe's eyes left Mike edgy and fighting not to change color.

"I don't know any easterner who shoots like that," one hand called.

"That's 'cause you don't know no easterner a-tall," another drawled and the first grinned and admitted it.

Mike turned to Peso and led him to the watering trough. He could feel the gaze of a couple dozen pairs of eyes boring into his back.

"Oh, Carey," Sharpe said.

Mike turned but said nothing.

"Before you sign on there's just one thing." Sharpe's brittle laugh didn't fool

Mike one bit. "That's a good quarter horse and when we start herding and rounding up I'll take him. You can have one of those." He waved to the score of horses in the corral.

A low murmur from the watching hands strengthened Mike. So did his lawyer's warning. Without a word he gathered Peso's reins, turned him from the trough, and mounted.

"Where do you think you're going?" Sharpe's voice cut the still air like a Bowie knife.

Mike deliberately rounded his eyes. "I'll get a job somewhere else. No one but me rides Peso." He touched his heels to Peso's flanks but was stopped by Sharpe's voice.

"Just testing, Carey. Climb down. Nobody else touches Peso."

SEVEN

The new Mike Carey gloated with every nail driven, every improvement made to the Circle 5 ranch. Enchantment lay in each sunrise and sunset, in lazy evenings at the end of satisfying hard days and in the thunderclouds that gathered above the peaks. It still seemed impossible that he owned the Circle 5.

Yet more important to him than the knowledge he daily proved himself to his fellow cowboys was a return of the old companionship with his Lord. Mike hadn't realized the depth of his emptiness until one early evening when he rode Peso to the knoll above the ranch and drank in the sweet night air. Now he whispered into the gathering purple shadows, "Thank You, God . . ." and left unsaid those things in his heart too deep for words.

Another day he faced the wild wind, rejoiced in the magnificent thunder and lightning, and then raced for the warmth and safety of the bunkhouse. Snowflake-sized raindrops pounded the earth and filled the air with the pungent fragrance of crushed sagebrush.

At first the Circle 5 cowboys drew an imaginary line with Mike alone on one side. To his amazement, few of the tricks he'd expected came. The second night Mike and the hands slept out when driving strays from the draws. Mike awakened to feel a gentle tug on his blankets. He opened his mouth to yell, remembering the campfire talk of coyotes so bold they sneaked into camp and dragged off blankets. Red-faced, lovable Joe Perkins had warned, "Coyotes out here sometimes get rabid. If ever you feel your blankets a-movin' just holler and we'll come a-runnin'."

Just before Mike hollered loud enough to be heard back in Concord, he remembered something else, the hastily concealed snicker followed by a glare at the boys from Joe. Mike clamped his lips shut and quietly investigated. His searching fingers discovered a taut rope. In a lightning move, he leaped from his blankets and with a mighty heave jerked the rope. Joe Perkins lurched then fell almost at Mike's feet, still holding the rope.

"What the —" A dozen cowboys sat up in their bedrolls. Mike couldn't tell in the starlight whether they had been rudely awakened or merely feigned surprise. He leaned down, helped Joe to his feet, and cried, "Thanks, pard! If you hadn't lassoed that doggoned rabid coyote I'd be foaming at the mouth soon." He whacked the ludicrous figure on the back. "Boys, I never knew how grand you were until now. I'll just bet you've been doing night watch for me all along." He stretched his mouth in a wide yawn. "That ornery old coyote's probably still running so we can all sleep better." Shaking with concealed mirth at the significant silence around him, Mike rolled up in his disarranged blankets and seconds later emitted a series of loud snores, his ears alert to the low rumble among the cowboys.

"I'll be hanged!" Joe's hoarse whisper faithfully carried his chagrin. "Think he really thought that? Or is he smart?"

"Mebbe both," someone else answered.

"Makes a man feel lower than a jackrabbit's belly to pull meanness on a man who *thanks* you for it," a third grunted.

"No more sneakin' around at night for me," Joe promised. "It's a wonder he didn't shoot! You all saw what happened the day he rode in."

Again Mike silently thanked God for steadying his hand on that momentous occasion. Only to Nate, who had carelessly ridden out and passed the time of day with the boys then managed to get Mike aside for a few minutes, had the new ranch owner confessed his shock when that bullet went straight.

Outside of a few other obviously half-hearted attempts that Mike's keen senses sniffed out and foiled, the boys abandoned attempts to make his life miserable. Joe did annoy Mike by sometimes attempting to imitate the eastern twang in Mike's speech but threw up his hands in defeat when Mike innocently said, "You sound kind of funny lately, Joe. Are you feeling all right?" He later overheard another just-among-the-hands conversation where the men unanimously agreed "twasn't no fun pesterin' a feller who don't seem to know when he's bein' funned."

All Mike's good nature combined with his innocent expression soon sponged the imaginary line. Yet a single incident welded him solidly into the chain of loyalty among his comrades. Hot, dusty, and wearier than he'd been in his life, Mike and the others rode into the ranch late one Saturday afternoon. According to range custom, they were free over Sunday except for those who had the misfortune to draw night duty. Mike could barely wait for Sunday. So far he hadn't been off the ranch or surrounding area but now he could attend church in Antelope and meet the Birchfields, and Desert Rose. His pulse pounded and he admitted that every step he and Peso had taken in the time he'd been at the Circle 5 had more or less been directed to that end.

Fate in the person of Dan Sharpe decreed otherwise. Mike knew without being told the foreman had taken a blind, unreasonable dislike to his new hand. Mike gritted his teeth and prayed his way through the dirtiest range jobs assigned to him. He would not whimper. He also realized for the first time how loving your enemies left them speechless. Although Sharpe well hid his feelings, the loud "haw-haws" of his men when Mike blandly raised his innocent blue gaze to his boss and whistled over his work rankled him.

"Why'd you let him put it over on you?" Joe Perkins demanded of Mike once when Sharpe had been particularly overbearing.

"I want to keep my job on the Circle 5." Yet Mike caught the doubt and disappointment in his new friend's eyes and inwardly sighed. Must he sacrifice the hard-won respect of his trailmates because Sharpe spurred him?

Prayer emboldened Mike for the next brush with his boss. When Sharpe arrogantly strolled into the corral where the tired hands were unsaddling and rubbing down their equally tired horses, Mike's lips set in a straight line.

"Oh, Carey, there's a bad break in the south pasture fence. Too late to fix it tonight so you'll have to do it tomorrow." The amber eyes held watchfulness.

Perkins slapped dust from his jeans with his hat. "Aw, boss, have a heart. Mike's put in the last two Sundays doin' chores."

Sharpe quelled him with a lightning glance and the other hands shifted uneasily or kept busy with their horses.

Mike slowly turned from Peso. "When did you learn about the fence break?"

"Yesterday, but what does that matter? I gave you an order. You'll get out there at daybreak and fix that fence." Sharpe's eyes glowed with anger.

"Why didn't whoever found it fix it?" Mike laughed and rounded his blue eyes. "Seems funny for someone just to ride in and say the fence is broken instead of repairing it."

"Fix the fence or get your time," Sharpe

snapped and strode away. His boot heels rang on the hard earth.

"I don't believe the fence is even down," Perkins burst out. He eyed the amount of light left in the sky, calculated, and swung toward Mike. "How about us takin' a little ride?"

"Right now? I thought you were going into Antelope with the boys." Mike thoughtfully glanced at the western sky as Joe had done.

Perkins scuffed his boots. "Do you want to go or don't you? I kind of hanker to see that fence for myself."

"Sure, but I won't take Peso." He slapped the quarter horse on the rump and Peso lazily ambled off to graze.

Joe grunted agreement. They chose fresh mounts from the bunch in the corral and fifteen minutes later headed toward the south range, chewing on biscuits filled with chunks of beef provided by the accommodating cook.

"Well, she's down all right." Joe reined in when they reached the fence. He slid from the saddle and carefully examined the pulled-up stakes. "Hmmm."

Mike joined him. "What is it?"

Joe tilted his big hat farther down over his eyes and drawled, "It either took a buffalo, a mean steer, or a man with a lasso to pull

113

up those stakes."

"Meaning. . . ."

"Meaning I don't know many buffaloes or mean steers who up an' jerk out a dozen posts all in a row just to be doin' somethin'." His lips narrowed to a slit. "Well, let's put 'em back where they belong." He pulled on heavy gloves and grimaced. "Nothin' a poor cowpoke likes better on Saturday night than fixin' a derned fence!"

Hours later the two rode home through a silver night so incredibly beautiful Mike wished he could just settle down for the night and watch it change from moment to moment. At Joe's suggestion, they had chosen a shortcut that took them off Circle 5 land and across a chunk of property between the Browns' Double B and Hardwick's Lazy H. Suddenly Perkins's low warning halted Mike.

"Somethin' funny here," Joe whispered. "There ain't supposed to be lights on that parcel. It's never used 'cept by the Lazy H for grazin'. They pay fees to the owner, whoever he is." His arm shot out and gripped Mike's shoulder. "Stay here and don't make noise, no matter what." The next moment Joe slipped off his horse and vanished into the dark shadows cast by trees and kissed by a night wind.

An eternity later a gunshot alerted Mike who still held the bridle of Joe's horse. It took all he could do to keep his own horse and Joe's from pitching. Then, silence. The moon had slid behind a cloud and Mike peered ahead. Joe had told him to wait but how could he, not knowing what that shot meant? With a quick prayer for guidance and help, Mike sprang from the saddle and tied the horses to a nearby tree. He couldn't take the chance of leaving them with reins standing as nervous as they were. No lights penetrated the darkness when Mike crept forward.

What seemed like a mile was in reality a few hundred feet between the horses and the point where Mike stumbled over something in the path. His heart leaped to his throat. Long, dark, and grotesque, a figure lay motionless at his feet. "Joe?" Mike dropped to his knees, felt for Joe's heartbeat, and his hand came away wet and slippery. He smelled it — blood.

The sympathetic moon crawled from behind its cloud and shone directly on Joe's pallid face. His eyes opened. "Pard, get outa here. Now! Five of 'em, they may come back." He struggled to sit up and fell back senseless.

Every instinct for self-preservation

screamed *run* in Mike's ears. He shook his head to clear it, snatched off his scarf, and jerked open Joe's jacket and shirt. "Thank God!" The wound he expected and found was high, away from the heart, near the hollow in Joe's shoulder. Mike stuffed the scarf against the seeping blood and ripped off Joe's scarf and wadded it against the gaping wound where the bullet had gone out of Joe's back. Perkins moaned and the pads shifted. Mike shed his jacket, tore his shirt into strips, and bound the life-saving pads into place then forced Joe back into his shirt and jacket.

Every ounce of Mike's newfound strength, and a broken, "God, help us, please," sustained him. Once the bandages lay firm, he considered then crept forward. He must ascertain that Joe's attackers had gone before attempting to move the cowboy he had learned to admire and love. Only the faint *thud, thud* of hooves fading in the distance could be heard. "They must not want anyone to know who they are or what they're doing," Mike surmised. The silver night had become the stuff of which nightmares are made. Somehow Mike got Joe into the saddle of his horse. Yet he reeled until Mike knew he'd never stay upright. They'd have to ride double and put the second horse on a lead line. If only good old Peso were here instead of this strong but flighty stallion!

Streaks of dawn caressed the sky by the time Mike and his injured companion reached the Circle 5. With his last spurt of energy he got Joe down and into the bunkhouse. Willing hands who had awakened from what little sleep they had after getting home late from the Antelope saloons fumbled and proved more bother than they were worth. Mike sent the soberest of the bunch to town for Dr. Birchfield and ordered the others to stand back. "We won't remove the bandages until the doctor comes," he told them. Bleary-eyed and unshaven, they bore little resemblance to the singing bunch who had come in from the trail dusty but eager for their night in town.

Disgust filled Mike. When he took over the Circle 5, he wouldn't stand for drinking. If it meant running the ranch with a half crew or doing it all himself, so be it. For an instant he wanted to rail at them all, tell them to look at what they were doing. His shoulders sagged, aching from the long night's strain.

"Pard?" Joe's weak whisper drove all condemnation away.

"Here," Mike triumphantly pressed Joe's hand. "Don't try to talk. The doctor will be here soon."

Joe's face wrinkled. His pain-glazed eyes looked around the bunkhouse. "Aw, you brought me home! How come you didn't save your own skin?"

Mike felt rather than saw the ripple of shock that froze the others around them. His voice rang. "Joe Perkins, if it had been I who got shot wouldn't you have done the same?"

A grin more like his usual look sat strangely on the pale face but Joe's eyes flashed. "Reckon I would." He licked dry lips. "Gimme some water, will you?"

The cook sprang to get it and Mike remembered something. "Did anyone tell Sharpe?"

"Naw, he rode out right after you did," someone volunteered. "Said he wouldn't be back until tomorrow. Didn't say where he was goin'."

Why did a strange feeling brush wings in Mike's mind? Too tired to identify it, he stumbled to a wash basin, cleaned up as best he could, and sat down to wait for the doctor.

His first impression of Dr. Adam Birchfield indelibly etched itself on Mike's brain.

Tall, dark, and authoritative, he said little while ministering to Joe except to state he had been given just the right attention and would heal in a short time. Not until he completed his work and washed his blood-stained hands did he turn his piercing black gaze that betrayed his relationship to Nate toward Mike. "New hand? I think Nate mentioned you." His grip proved to be everything and more Mike expected of the legendary man Nate had described. Mike met it squarely.

"Mike Carey."

"Have you studied medicine?"

"No, I just knew the blood had to be stopped. I prayed a lot, too," Mike added frankly.

In the paralyzing stillness that greeted his astounding announcement the tick of an old clock sounded loud. Then Dr. Birchfield said, "Well, thanks to *both,* your friend will be fine." He yawned and the black eyes danced. "I'd better get back to Antelope. Our population is due to be increased any minute and I'll be needed." He gripped Mike's hand again, nodded to the rest of the hands, and walked out.

"Can we get some shut-eye now?" someone plaintively asked and it started a rush to the bunks.

Hours later Mike came out of a sound sleep when the bunkhouse door crashed open and heavy-booted footsteps crossed the scrubbed wooden floor. "Where's Carey? Peso's here so Carey must be too. He's through. Any time I give a man an order and he ignores it — what's wrong with *you?*"

From the shelter of his blankets Mike grinned and waited for the fun to begin. He could see Joe propped up against a roll of blankets, his bandaged chest visible through a half-opened shirt.

"Well, boss, you'd be short one cowpoke if it weren't for Mike Carey," Joe drawled in his most maddening way. His hands curled around a cup of coffee and the steam spiraled up to hide his expression but Mike heard the glee in his voice and grinned again.

"Carey!" Dan Sharpe appeared absolutely flabbergasted. "Perkins, get that stupid look off your face and start talking."

With all the insouciance Joe possessed he began. "Me an' Mike thought we'd go on an' mosey down to the south pasture to the fence last night instead of him waitin' until today. See, he wanted to go to church, an' —"

"Forget what he wanted." Sharpe's eyes

looked more like a lion's than ever. "What happened?"

"We found the fence all righty an' fixed it. Funny thing about that." Joe's steady gaze bored right back into Sharpe's. "Anyway, when we got done the moon had come up so I said we'd cut through that piece of land between the Double B and the Lazy H."

"You *what?*" Blood poured into Sharpe's face and he made a quick convulsive movement that sent the same feathery tingle into Mike's mind that had been there the night before. Sharpe's hands clenched into fists. "What happened?"

"Don't know for sure." Joe scratched his head. "We saw some lights where they shouldn't have been. I told Mike to hold the horses an' I crept up toward the lights. I could see five figures."

"Recognize any of them?" A curious waiting settled on Dan's features and his knuckles showed white.

"Naw. Someone took a shot at me. Next thing I knew Mike was there stuffin' cloths on me. I told him to get out while he could. Didn't know but what those jaspers were hangin' around. He didn't. He packed me in."

From his viewpoint, Mike saw Sharpe's hands uncurl. The blood receded from his face, leaving it colder and more chiseled than ever.

"He must be dead," the foreman said disparagingly and glanced toward Mike's bunk where he lay prone, his eyes now closed.

"I ain't the lightest feller in the world," Joe said quietly. "An' it's a long way from where I got shot to the Circle 5. Besides, now that the fence's fixed, no reason why he shouldn't sleep, is there?"

With an inarticulate mumble Sharpe turned on his heel and slammed out the door. Its bang would have roused the dead so Mike opened his eyes, threw back his blankets, and sat up. "Joe? How's the shoulder?" He stretched and yawned.

"Sorer than the time I fell on a cactus." Joe's mouth twitched. "The boss was here. You get the rest of the day off. Too late for church, though. It's gettin' on toward three."

A pang went through Mike. He had really looked forward to attending church. "Maybe next week." He dressed, shaved, and ate a breakfast that even made the cook's eyes pop then decided to ride off some of his stiff muscles.

"Which direction are you headin'?" Joe demanded when Mike stated his plans for the afternoon.

"Thought maybe I'd ride back out the way we came home last night," Mike said casually but he knew his high color betrayed him. Would he never get over the childish trait of blushing? Must run in the family. Mercy had it too.

"Not until I'm able to go with you," Joe hissed. Mike turned to see the deadliest look he'd ever noticed in Joe's sharp gaze and Joe repeated softly, "Got that? Not until I go with you. Promise?" He held out his hand.

"Promise." Mike gripped Joe's hand and remembered what the Rock Springs lawyer had said about the Circle 5 cowboys. *Rowdy, lovable, ornery, soul-trying . . . once you pass their tests, they'll settle into a loyal crew who will stand behind you in high water and . . . its companion.* The look in Joe's eyes showed more plainly than words how that prophecy had come to pass.

EIGHT

A flurry of excitement greeted the Browns and Birchfields when they reached the church yard that Sunday morning. "Wonder what's happened?" Rose craned her neck to see. "Nate, help me down, will you? How I detest dresses!" She pushed down the bothersome skirts and smoothed her hair. Laurel insisted that she either wear it in curls or put it in braids on top of her head for Sunday and Rose hated that as much as the dresses.

"Did you hear the news?" a friend gushed. "Your father got called out to the Circle 5 early this morning. Joe Perkins got shot by unknown riders and the new young man we've been hearing about — Mike something — bandaged him up and got him to the ranch."

"The way I heard it is that this new hand is making a name for himself. Seems the first day he got there he put on a demonstration of shooting that convinced the hands he might talk like an easterner but he sure could shoot western!"

"What new hand is that?" Rose whirled on Nate. "Why don't you ever tell me anything interesting? Not that I care about any old cowboy," she added, then whispered in Nate's ear. "After all, *my* Michael is above showing off to impress people."

"How do you know?" Nate's black eyes twinkled.

"I just do." She smirked and adjusted her collar. "Drat this dress." She swept into the church with a chuckling Nate right behind her. "Oh, dear." She stopped short. Just ahead of them stood Columbine, her hand in Dan Sharpe's. Color came and went in Columbine's face, set off by her simple blue and white gown.

"Mr. Sharpe." Not a trace of emotion colored Rose's greeting. Unperturbed, the dapper man released Columbine's hand and smiled at Rose. "Miss Birchfield, Nate." He inclined his head toward the girls' glowering cousin. "I was just asking Miss Columbine if you young ladies and your cousins would like to ride over to the Circle 5 and —"

Rose started to freeze him with an "Impossible!" but she quickly reconsidered. Once

Columbine thought her family was persecuting the foreman her romantic notions would swell into a situation worthy of the Montagues and Capulets.

Nate had no such qualms. "I think Dad's about ready to start. Why don't we discuss it after church?" He adroitly escorted a reluctant Columbine into a nearby pew, then Rose, before placing himself on the end.

If Dan Sharpe saw through the move he didn't let on. "After church, then," he murmured and skillfully placed himself in a pew just ahead and across the aisle where Columbine's admiring gaze couldn't help focusing on him.

It took all of Rose's concentration to overlook the arrogant man and listen to the sermon. On this Sunday Reverend Nathaniel Birchfield had chosen to speak about loving your enemies and praying for those who despitefully use you. Rose frankly admitted in her heart, "Dear God, if I prayed for Dan Sharpe it would be for You to remove him to another range and *then* soften his heart!" The next second shame filled her. Quick to anger, she struggled for the meekness she knew God required of His children. "I'm sorry, God." She quickly added a postscript to her unspoken prayer.

"It's just that Columbine acts so fascinated and Dan Sharpe's more than twice as old as she is plus a million times older in experience." Rose turned her head slightly and love mingled with impatience for her sister brought moisture to the long, downcast lashes.

Columbine looked so demure, yet her eyes told other tales when she cast glances across the aisle to the pew ahead. Rose involuntarily shivered. Never, never, never must Dan Sharpe win Columbine! Dared she herself go back to the plan to attract him? She set her lips firmly. If that is what it would take to open Columbine's novel-blinded eyes, so be it. The rest of the sermon, closing hymn, and prayer blurred while Rose gathered courage for the distasteful task ahead. When the congregation spilled out open doors into the sunny world, she had herself under control.

"About that visit, this afternoon would be perfect," declared Dan Sharpe from his position a step behind the girls.

Rose stuck her tongue in her cheek but forced a smile and an upward sweep of lashes worthy of Miss Columbine. "Our parents have strict rules about Sunday riding except to church," she told him. "Perhaps another time."

"How are the rules about Monday riding?" Dan asked. His sardonic look showed he would not be deterred.

Rose hesitated just long enough to feign modesty. "If Nate and Sam are free perhaps we can ride over tomorrow."

"I'll expect you. Don't bother with food. My cook will prepare dinner." He smiled, shoved his hat on his tawny hair and walked to his horse, his posture ramrod-straight.

"Isn't he just the most exciting man you ever knew?" Columbine whispered in her sister's ear, so low that only Nate caught the words.

"He's one of the most dangerous men I ever knew, little cousin." Nate's black eyes flashed as he glared after the retreating Dan Sharpe, impressive as always on his beautiful buckskin. "If you have a brain in your head you'll stay away from him."

"How can I when he seems so devoted?" Columbine shot back.

"You ninny, can't you see he only pays attention to you when Rose isn't around?" Nate stood his ground.

A look of doubt crossed Columbine's face and Rose could have hugged Nate. Now that the seed of distrust had been planted, the elaborate scheme Rose had concocted to disillusion her impressionable and foolish sister could proceed.

Opportunity to further her intentions came the next day when the four cousins rode to the Circle 5. Although their foreman-host scrupulously treated the girls the same, Rose saw big-eyed Columbine watching every glance Dan Sharpe sent her way, measuring it against some inner yardstick. A few times Rose noticed Columbine biting her lip in vexation and the glow her younger sister wore like a cloak faded. Rose secretly rejoiced.

All the crosscurrents didn't keep the Birchfields from enjoying their day. The open admiration of the Circle 5 hands who gathered for the midday meal restored some of Columbine's good humor. Near the end of it a bowlegged cowboy bashfully approached the grassy area a little distance from the cluster of men who had finished eating and gone back to work.

"Beggin' your pardon, boss, but Perkins is feelin' real porely. Might be some purty visitors would lift his spirits." The messenger stood his ground when Sharpe snapped back at him.

"Get back to work, Haley. The young ladies have better things to do than hold some cowpoke's hand who didn't have better sense than to get himself shot up."

Haley cowered slightly but he would not be silenced. "You might recollect Perkins was on his way back from doin' his job when he got shot up." Haley's bright gaze searched Sharpe and he added softly, "Seems to me a man like that deserves some considerin'." He backed away wrapped in the dignity of the range that falls on hard working men when they are in the right.

"I should fire that fellow," Sharpe muttered then laughed and shrugged. "If I did, I'd lose half the others and with all the work to be done around here. . . ." He hunched his shoulders eloquently, but Rose caught the glowing embers of resentment deep in the foreman's eyes.

"I don't mind at all visiting this man, Perkins, is it? If it will make him feel better, we should see him." Columbine prettily clasped her hands and a gentle blush tinged her face.

Rose saw Sharpe's scowl and quickly jumped up. "I don't either, Columbine. Mr. Sharpe, would you take us to him?" She mischievously added, "Remember what Reverend Birchfield said about visiting the sick? My stars, I didn't know we'd have the chance so soon!"

Defeated, Dan Sharpe silently led them to the bunkhouse. The door stood open and only one man occupied the large room.

"Perkins, Miss Rose and Miss Columbine came to say howdy." Sharpe's look at the injured ranch hand sent chills up and down Rose's spine. She hesitated but Columbine walked close to the bunk where the cowboy lay. "I'm Columbine and this is my sister Desert Rose," she told the feverish man. "Oh dear, you do look miserable." With the skill that always amazed those who only saw the flirtatious side of Columbine, she located the water pail and dipper with one glance, a basin and cloth with a second. She brought water and gave it to Perkins then bathed his face. "There, isn't that better?"

An ugly laugh from behind Rose warned her of the foreman's growing anger. She stepped to Columbine's side and slid a protective arm around her then said, "Mr. Perkins, we have to be going but I hope you get well soon."

Some of his usual spirit surfaced. "I sure will, now. An' I'm Joe, not Mr. Perkins." But he didn't waste much time on Rose. He looked back at Columbine with a glance that shouted he had been stricken for a second time when she ministered to him, and this time straight to the heart. Rose intercepted the startled recognition in her sister's face before a burning blush spread over her white skin.

Rose exulted, wanting to do a war dance of joy. Let her get interested in this young cowboy and she's bound to compare him with Dan Sharpe to Sharpe's disadvantage. Even sick and "feelin' real poorly," Joe Perkins was obviously quite a man.

Before they told Joe goodbye, curious Sam could not repress one question. "What happened, anyway?"

Joe suddenly looked older. He compressed his lips and Rose got the distinct impression he wasn't telling all he knew. "My pard Mike an' me were ridin' home. We crossed that section where Hardwick runs his cattle. Someone took a shot at me an' Mike packed me in."

"Mike?" Nate raised an eyebrow. "I don't remember meeting anyone today named Mike."

"Mike Carey. He's just been here a little while but he's done proved himself." Joe's eyes brightened. "Once you meet him, why, he just ain't easy to forget."

"We really do have to go," Rose reminded Nate. She smiled down at Joe then looked toward Columbine. "When you're feeling better come see us at the Double B. During the summer we're there more than at home in town." The spirit of mischief prompted her to add, "Mr. Sharpe comes by now and then. Perhaps you can ride over together."

Her remark backfired. When the little party got back outside, Sharpe managed to corner Rose for a minute. "I'll hand it to you, Miss Birchfield. Thanks for getting your little sister all soft and sympathetic toward Perkins." His lips curled in an unpleasant smile. "It will free me to turn my attentions to the girl I really admire."

A surge of disgust and anger opened Rose's lips, but a warning signal in her brain went off just in time. "We'll see about that," she said, mounting Mesquite in record time to get away from the Circle 5 and its domineering, overconfident foreman.

"He seems nice, doesn't he?" Columbine dreamily said and relaxed in the saddle.

"I think he's obnoxious, wicked, and sickening." Rose let off the steam that had been building ever since she first met Dan Sharpe.

Columbine jerked on her reins so hard her horse danced and nickered in protest. "Why, Desert Rose Birchfield, what a mean thing to say. And when you only talked to him for a few minutes. I declare, you get more peculiar every day!" She stared at her sister. "He seems like a perfectly pleasant boy and if you took such an unreasoning dislike to Joe Perkins, why did you up and invite him to come visit us?"

Rose hid her astonishment and smiled at Columbine. "Sorry, Columbine, I was thinking of someone else. Joe does seem nice and if I'm a judge of cowboys — and I should be after living around them all my life — he will come calling the minute he can ride again."

Did Columbine whisper, "I hope he does" or did Rose imagine it? She couldn't be sure, for her sister leaned forward, called in her mount's ear, and galloped ahead.

The long, lovely afternoon's golden edges had begun to dim when the little band rode across the needle-covered stretch that led to the bald knob overlook and home. Nate and Rose had taken the lead with Columbine and Sam trailing a little behind. Glorious splashes of rose, red, orange, and pale violet stained the sky and reflected in the handsome faces of the riders.

Rose turned from the burning sky to the overlook point. Surprise straightened her spine. "Someone's there." Her brows knitted. "Why on earth would a lone rider be here at this time of day?"

"Come on, we'll find out." Nate hallooed and the figure turned. Rose gasped. Bathed in the sunset glow, a man stood etched against the far peaks in clean, clear lines.

The distance between the riders and limping figure diminished. Rose's observant eyes showed a man about Nate's height but a little stockier, a rueful grin spread across a good-natured face, lupine-blue eyes, and a shock of curly golden hair escaping from beneath a worn sombrero.

"Hello! I seem to be in your territory."

The unfamiliar accent didn't belong to Wyoming yet Rose found it pleasant.

"Nate and Sam Birchfield and our cousins Columbine and Desert Rose," Nate quickly identified. "Looks like you took a bad spill."

"It wasn't Peso's fault," the stranger quickly replied. Rose liked the defensive and affectionate way the cowboy glanced at the quarter horse standing a little way back from the promontory. "I got so busy watching that special display of God's handiwork —" He waved toward the ever-changing sky. "I didn't pay attention and Peso stepped in a gopher hole." The boyish laugh made Rose's lips twitch in sympathy. "Next thing I knew he was standing there and I was lying on the ground looking up at him. By the way, I'm Mike Carey."

"Really?" Rose flushed, disgusted at her involuntary response. "We just came from the Circle 5 and Joe Perkins mentioned you. . . ." Her voice trailed off in embarrassment.

"He tends to exaggerate the little service I did for him," Mike said matter of factly, rubbing his leg with a dusty hand.

"Are you badly banged up? Can you ride?" Nate asked.

Carey looked surprised. "Sure I can. I just figured as long as we were stopped I'd enjoy the scenic view for a while before heading back to the ranch."

Rose stared at the pinkened glaciers on the high peaks and the purple shadowed valley. "You called it God's handiwork. You must be a Christian."

The disappearing sun turned Mike's hair to burnished gold. "Yes, except for a time I —"

Nate interrupted. "It's good to meet you, Mike." His face shone in the wavering light. "We have to get home, though. Ride over to the Double B when you can. I'd like to have you meet Grandpa and Grandma Brown."

Mike Carey's steady gaze fixed on Nate. "I had planned on coming to church yesterday but it didn't work out. I will, the first Sunday I have off." He smiled a singularly sweet smile at the girls and grinned at Sam. "It's quite a ride back to the Circle 5 so I'll be on my way." He limped to Peso, mounted, raised a hand in farewell, and rode out of sight.

Quiet Sam, who now and then stunned his elders with rare bits of wisdom, observed, "He sure doesn't act like most of the cowboys around here. How many of our hands would get pitched off a horse and just sit on the ground looking at the mountains and sky?" He shook his head. "Something funny about him."

Nate exploded in much the same way Columbine had when she thought Rose was criticizing Joe Perkins. "Funny! Why say that? Is there any law that says a — a cowboy can't appreciate Wyoming scenery, 'specially when he's a Christian?"

"No law," Sam returned good-naturedly. "It's just not usually done in these parts."

The girls laughed and Nate couldn't help joining in. Sam's droll face became shadowed, reminding them of the miles still to traverse before they reached the Double B.

Once you meet him, why, he just ain't easy to forget. Joe Perkins's evaluation of the new hand floated in the graying twilight air and Rose found herself defending him, even as Nate had done. The look in his deep blue eyes revealed the cowboy's unwillingness to be praised for bringing Joe in amid adverse circumstances *and* the reverent way he had given God credit for the world around them. Yet Sam was right too. Mike Carey fit no mold that turned out cowboys. Where had he come from? Had he drifted up from Arizona or Colorado, perhaps away from a past that pursued him? There had been something in the way he confessed that for a time his Christianity — what?

Rose took comfort in the thought that whatever it might be, evidently he had worked through it. The next moment she grew disgusted with herself. Why should she care about a chance acquaintance? True, Nate had invited Mike Carey to visit the Double B, but she didn't have to waste time on him or any cowboy.

Her breath quickened. It had been some time since she had received a letter from Carmichael Blake-Jones. Now *there* was a man worth dreaming about if she were a girl like Columbine, always conjuring up romance behind every tumbleweed. A new realization came to her. No wonder she had been interested in Mike Carey. The moment she heard his name it reminded her of Michael.

She laughed aloud and wouldn't explain why when Nate asked her what was so funny. Imagine comparing polished Carmichael Blake-Jones with the dusty, limping, inattentive Mike Carey. She laughed again for pure joy. How wonderful it was that out of all the young men in the world, Michael had answered the advertisement! Would he ever include a visit to her Wyoming home in his travel itinerary?

Rose felt a blush start at the open collar of her soft riding shirt and lazily spread to her temples. How would she feel if he came? Would he love and appreciate the country of her birth, the hardships and glories, tragedies and hard work that sometimes left her feeling caged yet held her in a grip of iron? Would he gaze from the promontory and feel the thrill that swept through her each time she went there, the same awe she had seen mirrored in Mike Carey's blue eyes when he openly recognized God's handiwork? Or would Carmichael Blake-Jones be untouched, unable to look beneath the surface to find beauty in a raw and far from civilized land?

Rose's earlier joy dwindled and a feeling of depression rode side-saddle with her in the last few miles home. Deep in her heart she prayed: *Dear God, it would be better for him never to come than to compare my home — and me — to his eastern ways and friends. I felt You led just the right one to answer my advertisement, but perhaps You only mean for me to have a friend far away.*

She hesitated, longing to add as she had

been taught, "Thy will, not mine, be done." Instead she whispered so low even Nate couldn't hear her. "I don't know why, Lord, but I can't say it and be honest." For long, sleepless hours that night Rose sat by her window, stared into the silver world and wondered why.

NINE

The photograph had not done her justice.

Mike Carey carefully withdrew from his pocket the well-traveled photograph Nate had sent of Desert Rose and the duplicate she had mailed to him at his request and studied them. The spiritual quality of her face, the glistening auburn braid, the tanned skin, and her taunting dark brown eyes Mike Carey had just seen for the first time.

Neither had the photographs shown the litheness of her body, the charm of her smile, or the strength of hands that held her horse's reins lightly but yet with total control.

Burdened by his guilt, Mike's face contorted. If he had realized the power of her glance to penetrate his soul, would he have agreed to Nate Birchfield's mad scheme? His mobile mouth stretched into a wide smile that seemed to lessen the guilt. "I'm afraid I would have answered even sooner," he confessed to Peso, who obligingly whinnied in agreement. Mike carefully rewrapped the photos in the little square of oiled silk that fit in his breast pocket and kept them free of sweat and dust just above his heart.

August had become a series of memories. The hard work continued, as did Mike's battle of wits against Sharpe who seemed determined to make him quit. A few encounters with the Birchfield cousins on the range had resulted in an invitation to the Double B with a lovestruck Joe Perkins who stared at Columbine the entire time and announced on the way back to the Circle 5 that he intended to marry her as soon as he could!

By mid-September fall roundup was underway as well as plans for Columbine's sixteenth birthday. With the starting of school, she and Sam had gone back to their parents' home in town but Rose and Nate continued to spend a great deal of time on the Double B. Mike and Joe had been invited to the party in the big white frame house outside Antelope that Dr. Birchfield had built for his family several years earlier but neither had been able to attend. Black-faced with rage, Joe privately branded Dan Sharpe with several choice names when he sent the two out on night duty the afternoon of the party.

"Can't stand havin' competition," Joe said bitterly and slammed one fist into the palm of his other hand. His shoulder had healed quickly and his splendid strength put him back in the saddle long before Mike expected it.

Mike managed to hide his disappointment. "Which girl is he after? He's more than old enough to be their father."

Joe's jaw set and his blue eyes flashed fire. "Besides, there's stories about him and a woman in Rock Springs —" He broke off and dull color rose in his already-red cheeks. "He can play the gentleman all he wants but it don't make him one. As for which girl he's after, I've been figgerin' it out. 'Pears to me he wants Miss Rose but she acts like she ain't interested even when she's bein' friendly. Now her sister's different."

"How?" Mike couldn't help smiling at his cowboy philosopher friend.

"I know she likes me," Joe said without conceit. "But there's somethin' in her eyes when she looks at Sharpe that plumb scares me. I once saw a little girl look that way when she faced a rattlesnake, kinda fascinated-like in spite of herself."

"What happened?" Mike demanded.

"Why, I just up and shot the snake to save the girl." Pure devilment replaced the shadows in Joe's eyes and Mike threw up his hands but didn't forget the story and its ending. He couldn't blame his partner for being attracted to Columbine. At sixteen, her fragile beauty matched her name. Yet Mike suspected the same hardiness that permitted wild columbine to survive the elements and still raise its beautiful head existed in the budding woman.

"Any more words of wisdom in that noggin of yours?" Mike asked. He wanted to add *especially about Desert Rose* but held back. If Joe Perkins once got onto him, Mike's peace would "vamoose" the way Joe complained the ornery cattle did at roundup time.

Joe cocked one eyebrow and grinned. "I hear this party won't hold a candle to the one Doc and his wife are throwin' for Miss Rose in early November." Satisfaction brightened his face. "Roundup will be over an' everythin' snugged down for winter. We'll be right there with shinin' faces an' our company manners to help ree-joice that Miss Rose is eighteen." He heaved a long, deep sigh. "Before then, though, we've gotta round up some critters. Can't understand why Sharpe's sellin' now. The way I heard it, the new owner wanted to get more cattle, not less. Sharpe'll probably buy in the spring but it smells funny to me."

A thrill of danger and warning kept Mike from giving away that the owner of the Circle 5 couldn't understand, either. Should he contact his Rock Springs lawyer? Mike shook his head in answer to his own question. He'd watch and wait.

Nothing had prepared Mike for autumn in Wyoming. Although he came from an area of hardwoods that put on a spectacular and colorful show in the fall, it in no way overshadowed the spectacle he now rode through daily.

It's hard to describe, he wrote to Mercy. *Maybe it's the distant mountains that make the difference or the shining streams. I never dreamed I'd see anywhere as wonderful as New England when the leaves turn but Wyoming is just as grand.*

Mercy's reply came in a few weeks. *I'm so glad it's beautiful there too. How's our house — and my room — coming? I'm already working on Father and Mother. By spring I hope to have worn them down to where they'll wire you and beg you to take me so they can get some rest.*

Mike laughed over her letter but thoughtfully considered her question. He could find no fault with Sharpe's management of the Circle 5 except so far nothing had been done toward replacing Old Man Turpin's cabin with a more substantial house. The cabin had been reroofed and chinked against the coming winter. The bunkhouse offered comfort and warmth. The barn and corrals and fences stood in mute evidence to hard work. Once Mike casually asked Joe, "Isn't the boss going to build a house? Seems to me I heard rumors the eastern owner might visit come spring. I doubt he will want to bunk with Sharpe."

Joe just grunted. "I saw some plans stretched out on the table in the cabin when I had to see Sharpe one day. He musta noticed me lookin' at them 'cause he said someday the Circle 5 would be the finest ranch with the biggest an' best home on it anywhere near Antelope." He tapped his thumbnail against his teeth. "After roundup we'll probably get stuck with cuttin' trees if Sharpe plans to get a house started before the snow flies."

As if on Joe's schedule, the day after the roundup ended, Sharpe called the hands together. "You all know there aren't enough cattle left on the Circle 5 to keep you on over the winter." He paused and Mike glanced at Joe, glad his friend had told him how things were on the range in wintertime.

Sharpe shoved his hands against his hips and continued. "I can use any of you who want to quit for the winter and come back in the spring when I rebuild the herd. Now's the time for a nice, long vacation if you want one." His smile held little real amusement.

"I'll keep on those who are willing to cut and haul logs, lay floors, and play carpenter."

The men looked at each other and one older man said, "Not me, boss. I'm a cowpoke and it about killed me just fancying up the barn and fences and corral."

"Same here," others agreed.

"Fine. Pick up your time and I'll see you back in the spring." Sharpe stood waiting, his amber eyes half closed. "Any takers on my building offer?"

Mike shoved a sharp elbow in Joe's ribs. Joe glared at him, caught the silent signal in Mike's face, and in an offhand voice said, "I don't mind stayin'. I've got kinda used to my bunk."

A few others grudgingly muttered they'd stay, mostly older men who had wives and kids in town and rode in when they could.

"How about you, Carey?" Sharpe's question came just a shade too casual. "I suppose you'll want to look elsewhere for a winter vacation spot."

He might as well have added, *and don't come back,* but Mike chose to ignore the underlying message. His response was typically cheerful in the way he had learned stuck a saddle burr under his boss. "I'm with Joe. Say, Cookie's staying, isn't he?" Mike grinned at the rotund cook who served as the best advertisement of his culinary skills. Cookie grinned right back and nodded.

"I always hankered to see a house built out of logs that had to get cut down," Mike finished and bit the inside of his cheek to keep from roaring at Sharpe's barely concealed fury.

"Decided." Sharpe yanked his gaze away from Mike and jerked his head toward the cabin. "I'll pay off you who are leaving." He led most of the men away and the others dispersed, leaving Joe to grumble.

"How come you done volunteered me to cut trees? You know anythin' about it?"

"Not me." Mike threw back his head and laughed a ringing laugh that brought a scowl to his friend's usually cheerful countenance.

Joe looked toward heaven as if seeking patience and help then hissed, "Are you up to somethin'?"

Mike stopped laughing. "Look, pard, if we light out we'll have to hole up somewhere for the winter. How much of your wages have you saved?"

"Some." But Joe's scowl disappeared.

"If you're going to impress Dr. and Mrs. Birchfield as a suitable candidate for their youngest daughter's hand you can't do it broke," Mike said. "Chances are if we wintered in town you'd end up hanging around the saloons playing cards, maybe getting shot up, certainly broke by spring. Staying on the Circle 5 means good food, a warm bunkhouse, and wages all winter."

"But I hate choppin' an' cuttin' an' poundin'." Joe turned a tragic gaze on Mike and spread his hands out helplessly.

Mike fired his strongest shot. "Think what a good impression you'll make on the Birchfields. How can they, especially Columbine, resist a sober, hard-working cowboy who turns his back on idleness and evil and proves himself worthy to call on them when we aren't snowed in?"

"You shore paint a pretty picture," Joe said sourly. He shoved his hat down over eyes gone speculative and added half under his breath, "Might not be so bad at that."

"We'll be riding in to church and —"

"Church! I ain't set foot in a church since

149

I got to the Circle 5." Joe suddenly shoved his hat back and stared at Mike.

"Then it's time you did." In a single heartbeat Mike knew one of the finest things he could ever do would be to lead this wild, loyal rider to God. "Look, I don't say much because no one wants to get preached to in the bunkhouse but if you want a pardner who'll be there even when I can't, One who won't let you down no matter what, you'll start getting acquainted with Jesus. I've heard you tell a dozen times about someone you knew who fit your description of 'someone to ride the trails with'." Mike took a deep breath, then released it. "Try asking Jesus to ride the trails with you and I tell you, you can get through anything. I've never told a soul in Wyoming, but last spring both of my parents were killed in a railroad accident."

Mike ignored Joe's little movement and rushed on. "For weeks I took it out on God, blaming Him for not saving them. They were the emptiest weeks of my life. God hadn't turned away from me; I'd left His Presence behind me. It took a long time, and I still don't know why He let my folks die, but I know this: He loved me and you and everybody enough to send His only Son to die for our sins. He took our punishment,

Joe, and I'm going to keep Jesus as my trail-mate as long as I live."

Joe stood there thunderstruck. Mike half turned and said hoarsely, "Think I'll go for a ride."

Joe's quiet voice stopped him. "Think Sharpe will let us off Sunday?"

Mike nodded, too filled for words. He swung back and held out a work-hardened hand and grasped Joe's. Something in the steady blue eyes told him his witness for Jesus Christ had taken hold in the albeit rocky soil. Given time and patience, watered by friendship and prayer, God grant that it would grow and bloom.

Rose restlessly drummed her fingers on the table in the Birchfield living room. When Columbine, Adam, and Laurel all looked up inquiringly she burst out, "It's been ages since we went camping. Dad, can't you take a little time off? If we wait much longer it will be too late in the year."

Her father laid aside the medical journal he had been reading in a rare time of relaxation at home. His dark eyes thoughtfully reflected the maturity of all the years on the frontier. "Let's see, I don't have any mothers due to bring new life into the valley for a week or so. All the broken bones are healing well and, as far as I know, no one has scheduled any emergencies for a few days. Laurel, would it hurt Columbine to miss a few days of school?"

"Of course it won't." Columbine flounced herself closer to Rose. "I'm way ahead on my lessons."

Her mother's eyes sparkled. "I wonder if Nat and Ivy Ann and the children are free. Remember how wonderful it was when our families went into the mountains two years ago?" She glanced out the window into a perfect October day. "Rose is right. If we go it has to be soon. Look how low the snow is on the peaks, even though this is an unusually warm fall."

"This is Wednesday." Adam stood and stretched. "Why don't I walk over and see if the other Birchfields are interested? We can ride into the hills tomorrow and set up camp, stay over Friday, and come back Saturday in time for Nat to finish his sermon."

Laurel still gazed at the mountains. "I rather suspect Nat will be preparing his sermon the whole time we're gone — and what better place to feel close to God than in His beautiful creation!"

Adam couldn't resist teasing, "What if Sam isn't way ahead on his lessons?"

"He will be. He always is," Columbine said confidently. In the past few months she had begun to appreciate her quiet but fun-loving cousin and to develop a kinship with him similar to that shared by Rose and Nate.

Early the next morning the two families set out. In the years since Laurel and Ivy Ann came to Wyoming, their riding skills had become even more accomplished than when they rode the fields and hills near Shawnee, West Virginia. They stopped at the Double B just long enough to tell Thomas and Sadie where they were going and how long they would be gone, a frontier precaution. Wyoming in her gentlest mood still concealed a darker side waiting for those who failed to respect her many faces.

What a day to remember! Rose was in her element. Columbine left behind her airs and reverted to a simple girl who loved her family and the unexpected treat. The boys and their fathers talked of fishing and setting up camp, while Laurel and Ivy Ann shared the simple joy of being together.

By midafternoon the little band reached the spot Adam had selected after consulting with Nat. Few places among the crags offered such natural beauty, good water, and grass for the faithful horses. Soon eight pairs of hands had erected what Rose called HIS and HERS tents, spread bedrolls, started a fire, and begun preparations for a hearty camp supper. The sandwiches they had brought from home and eaten on the trail were only a memory as sizzling steaks, potatoes roasted in the ashes, canned peaches, and the cookies Columbine had found time to make before leaving Antelope were eagerly devoured.

By common consent, campfire talk turned to singing. Civil War songs and ballads gave way to hymns, and circled around the final embers of their fire, their hands joined, the Birchfields bowed their heads and Nat offered a prayer.

Love for her God, her family, and her country swelled within Rose. She could hear Columbine's quick intake of breath and feel Nate squeeze her fingers in a way that told they felt the same. Through the open flap of the tent Rose saw stars that looked close enough to touch and she fell asleep snuggled against Columbine with a prayer in her heart and her fingers against a letter that had come the day before.

Sometime in the night the drum of heavy rain on the tent awakened her. Columbine slept on but Rose slipped out of her blankets and let down the tent flap then mused for a time before falling asleep again. The second time she awoke the rain had stopped and she heard her father calling.

"Get up, everyone! We have to get out of here."

Fear clutched Rose and she shook Columbine awake. In record time the campers got dressed and hurried out into a gray dawn. "What's wrong, Dad?" Rose asked, trying to rub sleep from her eyes.

"I don't know and neither does Uncle Nat but we don't like it."

Rose followed his gaze to the stream nearby that had purled its welcome the day before. Now it looked muddy and sullen.

"With all this rain there should be more water in it," Adam explained. He looked up the stream to where it vanished around a bend. "Something is holding that water back, beaver dams, downed trees, maybe debris. When or if that something gives way, a wall of water will race down the stream bed and our trail is right alongside of it."

"What about going up and over?" Nate asked. Rose saw the concern in his face.

"Not enough food and no guarantee what the weather will be," his father said. "Hurry and get packed and mounted. Laurel, Ivy Ann, don't stop to cook. Do the best you can with whatever we can eat while we ride. Nate, Sam, girls, saddle the horses while

Uncle Nat and I pack the ponies. Wait!" He stopped them. "First we must pray."

This time fear ran through the circle even though Nat's calm petition for God's help restored Rose's normal heartbeat. After the *Amen* each person ran to break camp and in far less time than expected, the line of eight riders and two pack ponies had begun their descent of the mountain.

An hour later, the deluge came. Hastily donned slickers protected the riders to their knees but hats soaked through allowed streams of water to trickle down their necks. The winding trail became treacherous and slippery with mud. Even the horses so carefully trained to pivot and withstand obstacles found themselves sliding. Only the expert horsemanship of the riders kept them going.

The rain went on and on. "Think we should stop and build an ark?" Nate muttered.

Rose stifled a nervous giggle and Columbine sniffled. But the stream next to the trail continued to flow its even, muddy water. How long could this cloudburst continue and not sweep away even the firmest, most immovable obstruction?

"If we can make it five miles more, we leave the stream and go up," Adam encouraged. "From there we have a series of slopes and don't have to worry about a flash flood."

Down the trail they climbed, one mile then another. The rain didn't let up. Three miles, then four elapsed. Drop by drop the downpour lessened until Rose's heart beat high with triumph. Just one mile more! She patted Mesquite and the roan snorted and stepped over a slippery rock in the trail.

A half-mile from the junction where the trail and stream parted company they came to the narrowest place in the canyon. Rock walls on both sides frowned down on the wet riders even though the capricious skies had long since turned a deceptive blue shade.

"Watch the horses, ride as fast as you can without sacrificing safety, and God help us all," Nat ordered. He drove the pack ponies ahead at a fast clip. Laurel and Ivy Ann followed, then Rose, Nate, Sam, and Columbine, with Adam bringing up the rear.

Boom! The sound echoed down the canyon, and Rose tasted raw fear.

Ten

"Of all the miserable times to get caught out a thousand miles from nowhere, this beats everythin'!" Joe Perkins turned his coat collar up around his neck and glared at Mike Carey. "You an' your dumb idea to go huntin' while Sharpe's in Rock Springs."

"How did I know it was going to rain?" Mike defended himself and poked at the little fire in front of them that sputtered its protest against the storm. "Cookie said he sure could use some fresh venison so I told him we'd get some."

"An' dragged me along with you." Joe grunted. "We could have gone courtin' instead of spendin' the night out here." He waved at the blackness around the complaining fire.

"They aren't home." Mike didn't have to identify who *they* were. "One of the boys who rode in for the mail said he met Nate Birchfield at the post office and Nate said his folks and the girls and their folks were going camping in the high country for a couple of days."

"Why'd they want to do that this late in the year?" A little worry line crossed Joe's face and sent a quiver through Mike's veins.

"They probably didn't know it was going to rain, either," he reminded Joe.

"Who does in this country?" The worry line didn't go away. Joe tugged off his boots, turned them upside down over stakes he had driven in next to the fire and stretched his feet toward the little blaze. "Looks like the rain's letting up some. If we can get our socks dry maybe we can also get a little shut-eye. The tarps'll help." He waited until the drizzle stopped for a time and spread his tarp on the ground, waterproof side down. He tossed down the blankets that had been wrapped inside the tarps and finished by covering the hard bed with Mike's tarp, waterproofed side up. "I hope you don't snore."

"Only when I'm pretending to be asleep," Mike reminded, stifling a grin at the memory of the day Sharpe stormed into the bunkhouse spitting death and destruction.

Never in his entire life had Carmichael Blake-Jones, alias Mike Carey, spent such an uncomfortable night. He went to bed cold, stayed cold, and woke up a dozen times, still cold. It didn't help that Joe slept like a hibernating bear and only roused himself long enough to yank the tarp over their heads when the rain increased.

Along with his physical torment Mike couldn't help remembering the worry that creased Joe's forehead. When the gray dawn came, the stiff cowboys struggled into their boots. The fire had dried the inside a bit but the downpour in the night had soaked them again. "Why didn't you stick them under the tarp?" Joe asked. A trace of his permanent grin lightened the mood. "I'd have done it myself but I guess you noticed once I fall asleep it takes a lot to wake me up."

"I noticed." Mike let it go at that. Then he said, "Joe, uh, you don't think the Birch-fields would get into trouble, do you? They've lived here a long time."

"Only a fool or a newcomer tries to predict Wyomin' weather this time of year," Joe spit out. "Everythin' looks all bright an' beautiful like yesterday. Then along comes these innocent-lookin' puffy clouds that get their heads together an' the first thing you know, *bang!* You've got a storm." He eyed the sulky sky. "There's more to come. Did Nate say where they were headin'?"

Mike started to shake his head *no* then stopped. "Wait, I believe he did. Our rider said something about the gulch trail being the prettiest place around what with all the color."

Joe jerked erect. His apple-red cheeks lost their color. "Saddle Peso." He ran to Splotch, the pinto he liked best of the Circle 5 horses. "I reckon we'd better mosey along an' meet them comin' out."

Something in Joe's voice stilled the million questions knocking in Mike's brain. He forgot the rain, his growling empty stomach, everything except the fact the Birchfields might be in danger.

"Now's the time to pray to that God of yours," Joe said as he climbed into the saddle, wheeled Splotch, and touched him with his boot heels. "Come on, will you?"

Mike mounted Peso and in two jumps came even with Joe. "All right, pard, let's have it. It's worse imagining things than knowing how they really are." He had to raise his voice to be heard over the steady drum of the horses' feet.

"Couldn't be worse if they get caught on the gulch trail an' a wall of water comes racin' down." Joe's fixed gaze on their own trail didn't waver an inch. "It all depends on how far they went, how fast they started

161

out this mornin', an' if they got past the point where the trail leaves the creek." A steely gleam that crept into Joe's eyes when he glanced at him confirmed Mike's fears.

"How far are we from there?"

Joe grunted. "Far enough, but we're a derned sight closer than if we'd had to come from the Circle 5."

"Just maybe God knew we'd be needed and that's why we got caught out last night," Mike reflected.

"Maybe." Joe's lips set in a grim line and Mike lapsed into silence, pouring out his concern in an unspoken prayer.

An eternity later Joe called, "One more hill."

Panting from their run, Peso and Splotch scrambled to the top of the rise and plunged over, sliding on wet needles and grass.

Boom! A distant reverberation chilled Mike and Joe swallowed hard. Heedless of possible danger, they urged their horses down the slope.

Before the echoes died in the narrow canyon, Nat bellowed, *"Ride for your lives and don't spare the horses!"* He whacked the pack ponies with his leather quirt until they whinnied in terror and bolted down the trail. The others followed, slipping, regaining their balance.

How much time did they have before churning waters poured toward them? Rose wondered. She expertly guided Mesquite, conscious of Columbine's half-sobbing breath behind her and Nate's encouraging, "Steady, Piebald, easy." The half-mile to safety dwindled to one-fourth of a mile. The trail widened slightly and Rose's death grip on her reins loosened. The pack ponies were out of sight. Nat swerved his stallion to one side, close to the cliff, and motioned Laurel and Ivy Ann past, then Rose.

The vanguard of the flood waters reached them, a roiling, hungry monster seeking vengeance after being restrained miles above. *"Go, Mesquite!"* Rose screamed. He snorted, stretched out to his full length, and leaped away from the relentless tide. Laurel and Ivy Ann had reached the junction where the stream went one way, the trail the other, up an incline to a flat benchlike formation. Their weary horses forged ahead and stopped on top, trembling and spent.

A wall of muddy water hit the others like an avalanche. Mesquite swayed but kept his footing and nimbly sailed over a rushing log, staggered, then stamped his way to safety.

Rose turned and cried out in despair.

Below her the other horses fought valiantly. Piebald made it to the junction and raced toward the bench high above danger.

"Oh, dear God, please help them!" Rose couldn't tear her gaze from the awful scene. Logs, some upright, rode down the gulch, smashing this way and that. Nat's stallion stood braced against the rock wall, up to his knees in sucking water. "Head your horse this way," he shouted to Columbine. Her face shone paler than the flower whose name she wore but she tried to obey.

The next instant a branch grazed her horse's flanks causing him to rear. Columbine stayed in the saddle but Rose could see that her sister's strength had been tried to the utmost.

Nat's stallion went down. Adam's horse attempted to swim but the current made it impossible. To Rose's horror, her father disappeared in the sweeping torrent around the bend. Nat's magnificent animal regained his precarious position.

"Rose!" Columbine's pleading voice beat in her sister's ears but was replaced by pounding hooves and men shouting. Nat grabbed for Columbine, and missed, and his wild cry rose above the tumult. Both Nat and Columbine went under when the big stallion and the girl's mount stumbled and fell, to reappear, but unable to brace the flood.

Something sang over Rose's head and she whipped around. Joe Perkins had thrown his lasso. It fell far short of Columbine but close enough for Nat to grab it and be hauled in. Regardless of her own safety, Rose stumbled toward the edge of the bench. She couldn't just stand there and do nothing! Nate tackled her and brought her down. "You can't save her, Rosy. Only God can do that. Look, *look!*" he shrieked.

Mike Carey had urged Peso into the river. Strong and powerful muscles rippled in the quarter horse's shoulders. With his knees and left hand clenched to keep in the saddle, Mike's right hand readied his lasso. Then he, too, passed out of sight around the bend, leaving only the thundering flood to taunt the mortals shivering on the little bench of land.

Mike only had time for a quick prayer before entering the now river-sized stream. The moment he and Joe saw the trouble no question arose as to their duty. Mike waited long enough to see Joe's rope fall short of Columbine before he charged into the river, appreciating to the fullest the horse he rode. After that he had no thought for anything except getting to Columbine before a crashing branch knocked her out. When he surged around the bend and saw the girl clinging to the branch of a tree only God could have kept from crushing her, he gave a cry of joy. Yet Columbine remained in danger. How long could she hold on with the treacherous flood waters pulling at her?

Mike cast a quick glance ahead and again cried out. Downstream a stumbling figure at the edge of the water showed Adam Birchfield and his soaked horse making their way to safety. The gulch widened at that point but Mike saw how it narrowed again into what had to be a drop-off. "Dear God, I have to get her out here or not at all." His fingers tightened on his lasso. "Hold on, Columbine!" he yelled as loud as he could.

For the second time in Mike's life, another human being's life depended on him, and he knew as surely as when he had saved Joe, that he had to act at once. There would be no time to recoil his rope if he missed.

Peso gained on the frail craft that supported the girl and finally drew even. Mike screamed into the heavens, "Give me Your help, oh God," and threw the rope.

The rope missed the girl but caught on the branch she held. With daring born of desperation Columbine released one of her hands from the branch, lunged for the rope, and somehow got it over her slender shoulders. Mike saw her lips move while he tightened the lasso around his saddle horn. "Now, old man!"

All the breeding that made Peso the best roundup horse on the range sprang into life. Inch by inch he fought his way until he swam close to Columbine. Mike clasped his knees against Peso's heaving sides and, bending from the waist, scooped Columbine into his arms not a moment too soon. A purple bruise showed where floating debris had struck her. Her light brown eyes looked black with emotion.

"All over but the shouting." Mike tried to smile and saw her tears start. A few minutes later Peso gained the shore in spite of his double burden and Mike slid from the saddle, laid Columbine on his tarp, and hurried to where Adam lay gasping a few hundred yards away.

"Are you all right, sir?" He helped the dazed man sit up.

"Laurel, Rose, the others? Columbine? Oh, dear God, tell me they're not all dead." His prayer brought weakness to Mike's knees but he shook Adam until his eyes cleared.

"God has saved every one. *Every one,*" he repeated. "The others are back at the junction of the trail. Columbine's just below. Peso and I fished her out."

Adam still looked confused and Mike shook him again.

"I don't know if Columbine's hurt. She needs you to look at a bruise on her face."

The appeal for his God-given skills reached the doctor as nothing else could. With Mike's help, Adam limped downstream and grabbed Columbine into his arms.

Mike looked away, back at the flood waters that had already begun to abate until only muddy grass showed how they had spilled over their banks.

"I'll build a fire," Mike said. "If I can find dry wood."

"Do you have dry matches?" Adam's expert hands checked over Columbine to make sure no bones were broken.

"Always. A candle stub too." Mike found a sturdy branch from the flood, whacked open the trunk of a dead tree and scooped out the dry inside. Before long a tiny fire smoldered. A few soggy biscuits from the saddlebags offered sustenance.

"I expect the others in a few minutes," Adam said.

"The water is down and they can pick their way. What did I tell you?" He pointed upstream to where horses and riders gingerly came between discarded logs at the edge of the gulch. "Good. The pack ponies didn't get wet at all. We'll have hot food before long."

Rose's eyes looked like drenched brown velvet pansies when she saw Columbine sitting up against a saddle, bedraggled but safe. She gave a little cry. "We prayed so hard. Thank God. How did He save you? Joe Perkins dragged Uncle Nat out after his horse went down."

"He did?" The glory in Columbine's eyes sent a sheepish grin to the cowboy's red face. "Dad stuck on his horse and the flood swept him close enough to shore so he could get out. I thought I wouldn't make it when I lost my stirrups and the current got me." Stark horror returned and Rose hugged her but Columbine bit her lip and went on. "I grabbed a branch on a log that came toward me. Just when I knew I couldn't hold it any longer I heard a yell to hold on. Someone threw a rope and it caught the branch. I got it around me and then I don't remember what happened." Her dirty fingers explored the bump on her head. "I guess something hit me. Then I was in Mr. Carey's arms and he got me out and — oh, dear! I'm going to cry." The tears she had held back so long threatened to drown Rose, who still held her close.

"We couldn't believe that you'd leap into that flood," Nate told Mike. Color returned to his white face.

"I didn't stop to decide," Mike admitted and patted Peso's neck. "I'll tell you, if it hadn't been for God and this old man here —"

"Don't say it," Rose pleaded and tightened her hold on the sister she had never before known she loved so much until she almost vanished in the dirty, rolling waters.

Joe Perkins didn't say a word but Rose noticed how serious he looked when the others talked about God saving them. Her cold heart warmed. Maybe someday . . . she didn't finish her thought. Right now they needed to get home.

"We lost two horses," Adam said. "Columbine's and mine. There's a chance they'll get out somewhere below and come home but even if they don't, that's a small price compared with —"

"With what could have happened," Laurel finished quietly.

"We'll redistribute the pack ponies' loads onto the other horses and Rosy and I will ride them bareback," Nate offered.

"I'll ride a pack pony and Miss Birchfield

can ride Peso," Mike corrected, without looking at Joe Perkins who made a funny sound in his throat. Was he thinking of Mike's boast months ago that no one would ride Peso but his owner?

"After all we've been through this Mr. Carey and Miss Birchfield business sounds downright unfriendly." Nate's spirits had already bounced back.

"I agree if Miss, er, Rose does," Mike quickly inserted.

A lovely light shone in her eyes. "I do. Thank you for the loan of your horse, Mike." She stepped into the stirrups and stood while he adjusted them to her shorter height. "Now let's go home. Not to Antelope, but to the Double B. We can get dry there and Grandma will feed us." She paused. "That includes you two," she told Mike and Joe.

"Grub sounds good to me," Joe said heartily and a murmur of assent rippled through the stained but thankful band.

Hours later, in the crisp, clear evening Mike and Joe rode home to the Circle 5. Bright stars guided their way, yet none glowed more brilliant or beautiful than the girls' eyes when they told the cowboys goodnight and thanked them again. Mike didn't notice how much distance they had covered in silence until Joe heaved a sigh. "I reckon that trailmate of yours came in mighty handy today."

Mike's heart lurched with gladness. "I reckon He did," he repeated. When Joe didn't respond, Mike added, "He's waiting to be your trailmate, too, as soon as you invite Him along."

"I know." Joe sighed for a second time. "A feller'd be an ungrateful cuss for not acceptin' Him, wouldn't he?"

Mike reined in Peso their forms silhouetted in the starlight. "Joe, I'd give almost anything in the world to have you accept the Lord but it can't be just because he sent a miracle and saved the Birchfields today."

The pale light didn't hide Joe's astonishment. "Who said anythin' about that bein' the reason?" he demanded. "Didn't you say Jesus came to save everybody an' died to do it?"

"All those who believe and claim the promise." Mike didn't move a muscle. The night wind held its breath and the mountains loomed as if waiting for Joe to answer.

"Well, I guess if He wants a poor, sinful cowpoke who's sorry, I'm willin'." Joe rode away before Mike could recover his wits enough to realize what had just happened. How like Joe Perkins to confess his sins and invite Jesus to be his trailmate in his own unique way! A few long lopes and Peso overtook Splotch. Mike didn't say one word. He just held out his hand and gripped Joe's and sealed the brotherhood between them.

An errant thought that maybe someday they might truly be brothers in the eyes of the world as well crossed Mike's mind, a thought only shared with his loving and merciful Creator.

Eleven

Nate Birchfield never expected God to solve his dilemma by sending a flood down a narrow gulch and scaring the daylights out of him. All summer and into early fall he had sought God's guidance about going into the ministry. When it came time to think about returning East for school, Nate had to confess to his parents the reason he didn't want to go. If he lived a million years he wouldn't forget the look on his father's face.

"I — I feel like I might be called to be a minister but I need some time," Nate implored. "I have to be sure."

"We understand, son." Nat placed both hands on Nate's strong shoulders. "Unless God specifically calls you, you must never take on yourself this work."

All the time Nate rode and teased Rose, helped out on the Double B, and lay awake nights, his mind stayed close to his decision. Then on a soggy chunk of benchland above a death-dealing stream his answer came.

He could pinpoint the instant, the one that Columbine was swept around the curve and his mother screamed. Nat was still at the end of Joe's rope getting hauled in. With all his boyish heart Nate longed to comfort his mother but had no words. If only he were like Dad who seemed to say the exact thing needed for every occasion! All he could do was to put his arms around Ivy Ann and hold her until Nat finally reached the bench and took over.

The next day he sought out his father. "Dad, does being a minister tell you what to say when people need you?"

Wise Nat! He made no effort to explain things to his son in an easy way. "I believe God gives us the words but only after we have done everything we can to prepare, which means praying, fasting, and studying the Scriptures. It's like when your mother cans for winter. If she puts up fifty quarts of peaches, most of them probably won't be needed for a long time, unless you're around with your big appetite!"

Nate grinned but listened intently and his father went on.

"Learning the Bible verses is like that. It may be a long time before we need all of them." He paused and his face softened.

"But when you do, you know they're right there waiting," Nate said. "Just like the peaches."

"That's right. Yet times come when all our knowledge and wisdom fail. That's when the Holy Spirit steps in and guides our thick and stammering tongues." Nat's eyes glistened. "I believe you are very close to finding answers to your questions, Nathaniel. Be patient and don't try to rush God. He answers the way He chooses in the time He chooses." A kindly thump on his son's shoulder betrayed the father's joy and peace that had come with years of struggle and hard work.

Nate had never felt closer to his father. Gradually his questions ceased. Not that he had all the answers — he probably never would. Yet the growing knowledge of what trail God called him to ride became a certainty. A few days after the flood Nate and Rose rode to their favorite bald knob viewpoint. With Columbine and Sam back in school, extra chores fell on the older brother and sister and left less time for rides.

Desert Rose sat on the dry, needle-covered ground, her jean-clad legs pulled up, arms wrapped around her knees. The drenching rain had muted the once-gorgeous fall colors, creating a somber scene. "It's sad, isn't it, the dying of the year. Soon the snows will come and bury all this —" She waved at the rolling hills and mighty peaks.

"Yet we know that life in the trees isn't dead, just sleeping until spring," Nate reminded. He abruptly added, "How anyone who watches the seasons change and sees the dry, barren trees put on green after the snows and not believe in the resurrection of Jesus is beyond me."

Something in his voice turned Rose's dark gaze from the valley and mountains toward her cousin. Gladness filled her. "You've decided."

"I have." His unflinching face showed the hours of struggle that had changed him from a boy to a man. "I told my folks last night. It's all settled. After Christmas, I'm going away."

"Oh, no!" But Rose instantly regretted her selfish cry. She blinked hard. "I'm happy for you, Nate, really I am. It's just that I'll miss you. Where are you going?"

"Back to Concord and Grandpa and Grandma Birchfield's!" The quietest smile Rose had ever seen on Nate's face appeared. "I'll study hard until summer, come back here, then go for one more year. After that is up to God."

His reverent trust almost unleashed her tears but Rose valiantly held them back. She mustn't spoil this precious moment with foolish regrets. A new thought came. "Why, you'll see Michael!" Warm color swept to the roots of her hair.

"He isn't there, remember?" Nate changed to the laughing companion she adored.

"Well, he won't stay away forever, will he?" She flounced a few inches away from him. "My goodness, he will have to work again when his vacation is over."

Nate choked. "Oh, I can't imagine him not working." He grinned. "I'll wager that if he stays in a place long he will find some kind of job while he's there." Nate lay back with his head on his crossed arms and stared at the sky. "Rosy, have you ever been sorry you took my dare and wrote to *Hand and Heart*?"

"No." The word shot out. She nervously plucked at the button on her shirt sleeve. "I made a wonderful new friend."

To her mystification a look of — was it relief? — crossed Nate's face. "Then everything will be all right." He sprang up and gave her a hand and together they walked to the patient Mesquite and Piebald who stood with reins hanging. "By the way, have you seen anything of Mike Carey lately?"

To her annoyance Rose found herself blushing again. "Not since they came home with us after the flood. Why?"

"Just wondered." The teasing left Nate's eyes. "You like him, don't you?" he asked irrelevantly.

Rose stared at Nate. "Of course I do. Don't you? He's the nicest cowboy around and he doesn't make sheep's eyes at me the way most of them do. He must have been a gentleman to have such good manners."

A curious stillness settled between Nate and Rose that lasted until after they mounted and headed down the long slope toward the Double B. At last Nate said in a hard voice, "You think a cowboy can't be a gentleman? Isn't that a bit snobbish?"

Angry flares streaked Rose's face. "I didn't say that. It's just that Mike Carey is not like our Wyoming riders." She dug her heels in Mesquite's sides and he pranced away before her cousin could reply. Yet his question stayed with her. *Was* she guilty of snobbery, a trait she hated? Rose impulsively wheeled Mesquite back toward Nate. "I'm sorry, Nate. I guess some of the old South is in me, you know, the importance placed on family lineage and all that."

Nate visibly relaxed and his old friendly grin came out like the sun after a shower.

"Rose Red, you just need a strong man like me around to keep your feet on the ground."

"Don't call me Rose Red," she automatically protested but she couldn't hide the little smile his comment brought.

Hours later not even the whisper of a smile remained. The same brooding atmosphere that had hung over the Double B and other ranches in 1892 when the Johnson County Cattle War raged in north-central Wyoming plagued the ranches again. Rose remembered the newspaper accounts during that time. Cattlemen suspected their herds were being rustled but had no proof. Owners of the large ranches made a list of suspects, imported two dozen Texas outlaws, and formed a force of over fifty-five men called the Invaders. They raided the Kaycee ranch near Buffalo and killed two men.

When word of the killings reached Buffalo a group of armed men rode out after the Invaders and confronted them on the TA ranch but federal troops got there in time to prevent any slaughter. Although the Invaders stood trial in Cheyenne, witnesses didn't show. The Invaders were set free and the so-called war ended.

During that time Antelope breathlessly waited, armed and ready in case the violence spilled over into the little mountain hamlet that liked to call itself a town. When nothing extraordinary happened, the townspeople and ranchers got back to the business of daily living, but many remembered sleepless nights when the slightest noise brought husbands and fathers out of bed.

No one knew how or where but talk of a new band of rustlers now ran rampant. Folks who hadn't oiled up guns except for hunting took down their firearms in case they were needed. Grim-faced riders reported missing cattle and horses. Some told of seeing lights in uninhabited areas. Unease and furtive glances between formerly friendly neighbors increased the tension. Who could be trusted? Rustlers could be living right in the middle of honest people, masquerading as others had done under the guise of upright citizens. Even the approaching celebration of Desert Rose Birchfield's eighteenth birthday couldn't compete with the restless waiting.

On November 2, 1895, a light snow fell then surrendered to the late autumn sun. *Why don't I feel grownup?* Rose wondered when she awakened and hurried to her window. *Is it because everyone acts so worried?* A flash of perception stilled her fingers on the curtain. *Perhaps I don't want things to change.* She expressed that idea to her mother in a private talk later that morning.

Laurel smiled the contented smile of a happy woman but her rich brown eyes held understanding and memories. "I felt very much the same way twenty-two years ago," she confessed. Her beautiful hands, slim and graceful yet strong, lay idly in her lap. "Because the years after the war were so hard, Ivy Ann and I didn't have an eighteenth birthday party but oh, what a glorious celebration we had on our twentieth birthday!" She laughed. "I can't say it was the happiest night of my life but now I see it as a turning point. I had walked in my twin's shadow far too long and it wasn't good for either of us."

"Then Dad came." Rose loved the story.

"Yes." Dreams turned to joy but Laurel shook her head. "I'm afraid I had some very un-Christian thoughts toward Ivy Ann over Adam!"

"I wonder if I'd have the courage to do something as outrageous as traveling alone to Wyoming from West Virginia in a time when women wouldn't dream of such a thing?" Desert Rose mused.

Laurel cupped her elder daughter's face in her hands. "My darling girl, when you fall in love I shudder to think what outrageous thing you may do." Her gaze probed deeply into Rose's heart. "One thing I know, whatever that thing might be, I know that with your faith in your Heavenly Father you will never act in any way except an honorable one." She pressed her lips to Rose's tanned forehead then changed the subject.

"I know you don't like dresses but isn't your party gown lovely?" She glanced at the cobweblike white froth swaying gently in the breeze from Rose's open window.

Rose scrutinized the dress from its tiny, standup collar to its puffy sleeves and fitted bodice down the sweep of flaring skirt to the wide hem. "It's beautiful." She giggled. "But I'll never forget how outraged the dressmaker acted when I told her I would *not* be laced into an instrument of torture to make my waist smaller and that I would *not* wear any hourglass dress." Rose stretched and admitted, "She did a wonderful job, though. Since it's my first dress from a dressmaker, I'm glad. Besides, after I wear it tonight I'll pack it away and it will do for a wedding dress. I suppose whoever — I mean whomever — I marry will like it." She felt warmth all over when the name Carmichael Blake-Jones came to mind. *How would he react if he could see her in this white confection?*

Rose suddenly felt she was holding on to

childhood with one hand and mentally reaching toward womanhood with the other. *Please, God, don't let me . . . don't let me what?* Rose broke off her unspoken prayer and quickly substituted: *Just keep me strong and true to You. Make me worthy of my mother's trust, and Yours.*

The change from boyish, laughing rider to what Columbine labeled "a vision of loveliness" vanquished even the rumors of rustling from the birthday guests' minds. The moment Desert Rose donned the gossamer gown, so modest yet enhancing, and submitted to her sister's expert arrangement of her long, shining auburn hair, a certain wistfulness hovered in her eyes.

Mike Carey, resplendent in the dress suit some whim had included in his packing, couldn't keep his gaze off the slender figure that had taken on some of Columbine's deceptive fragility. Yet a feeling of loss for the thick braid of hair, jeans, and old shirt haunted him. Tonight Rose Birchfield bore little resemblance to the Desert Rose in the picture above his heart. He couldn't know how her pulse raced when she saw the transformation his dark suit made. Even for church Mike had clung to more casual attire so Joe, who now went with him, wouldn't feel outclassed.

Dan Sharpe turned out to be most thunderstruck. His tawny eyes gleamed above his sparkling white shirt front and dark suit. Alarmed by the predatory look in those eyes when he greeted her, Rose braced herself for his dreaded move. Immediately Dan turned to Columbine whose pale blue and white dress made in much the same style as her sister's set off to perfection her brown hair and light brown eyes. Although Columbine looked kindly on dashing Joe Perkins, some of the old dazzlement remained in her eyes when she faced the immaculately attired foreman.

Thomas Brown had taught the girls, "If you have a job to do, do it. No sense putting off hunting down a skunk if it's under your house and you have to get rid of it." The longtime advice lent courage to his granddaughter even though her lips trembled with unspilled laughter. How would Dan Sharpe feel if he knew she considered the next hour even more disagreeable than hunting down a skunk?

Rose didn't have to do much to encourage Dan. Just after the generous supper and cutting of the tall white-frosted layer cake with its eighteen candles, Dan whispered, "It's so warm in here. Will you walk outside, Miss Rose?"

"It is warm," she agreed and took his arm in spite of the dark look Nate sent her. She barely heard Sharpe's lavish compliments on how he had fallen in love with her until they reached a clump of cottonwoods.

Suddenly bands of steel pinned her arms to her side and Dan kissed her full on the mouth.

"Oh-h!" The soft sound effectively separated them. Unknown to Rose, Columbine and Joe Perkins stood a few feet away in the moonlight.

"You monster!" Rose forgot the role she played in a wave of fury. Her right hand lashed out and struck Sharpe in the face with such force he staggered. "Get off the Double B and don't come back, ever." For the moment, she didn't care about range hospitality that made such an order taboo. "Go! Do you hear me?"

Dan's left hand slowly went to his cheek. His eyelids half-closed over his eyes. "When a lady encourages a gentleman, she should expect what she gets."

Joe roared with rage and leaped forward, hampered by Columbine's clutch on his arm. She cried, "No, Joe. Don't ruin Rose's party." She looked appealingly at Sharpe, her only interest in him obviously to stop a fight. "You'll go, won't you?"

"Of course." Venom sprayed from Dan but he turned to Rose. "You'll regret this. I honestly cared for you, just as I did for your mother and her twin." He strode to where his buckskin waited, slid into the saddle, and rode away without a backward glance.

Rose's sense of fair play scorched her. Never in her life had she felt so unclean, so cheap. His unwelcome kiss lingered on her lips and she scrubbed it away with a lacy handkerchief. She couldn't scrub away her guilt. It didn't matter that she had tempted him to save her sister. Shame filled her like flood waters in a gulch.

Columbine ran to her and helped smooth her mussed hair and dress. Practical when expected to be helpless, she drew her sister around to the kitchen door, slipped inside, and brought water. Rose drank some of it and patted her burning face with the rest. She dried her hands and face on the big clean handkerchief Joe solemnly offered. "I'm ready to go back in now," she told them. Surely the excitement would cover signs of her heaving emotions.

Nate met them at the door. "Where's Sharpe?"

"He found out he had to leave," Joe drawled into the puddle of silence that greeted Nate's question.

Nate looked suspicious but Joe blandly stared him down.

"How about some music?" Columbine took charge and Rose longed to hug her. "If everyone will gather around the piano we'll sing. Now if all of you would come to church every Sunday we'd have quite a choir, wouldn't we?"

In the ripple of laughter that followed, Rose glanced around the room, seeking one face, one pair of reassuring blue eyes. "Why, where is Mike Carey?"

"Funny thing. He stepped outside a little while ago, came back in almost before the door closed behind him, and muttered something about having to get back to the Circle 5. He looked kind of sick. I asked him if he wanted me to ride with him or get Joe and he just shook his head and said he'd be all right." Nate's gaze never left Rose's face.

"Why didn't you have your father look at him?" Columbine demanded.

"It wasn't that kind of sick. He looked more like something had hit him square between the eyes."

Rose felt ice form in her toes. "He was only outside a few minutes?"

"More like one minute, or even thirty seconds." Nate shrugged and Rose bit back hysterical laughter. *What had Mike Carey seen in those thirty seconds?* Probably too much, and not enough. The kiss, certainly, but not the aftermath. In his one quick glance from the doorway to the cottonwoods he could not have seen her reaction.

All pleasure in her party died a quick and final death. Rose wanted to rip off the white gown, climb into her riding clothes, and head Mesquite away from the laughing throng.

Continuous prayers for forgiveness and the strength to survive until the last of the guests left kept a smile on the tortured girl's face. After cleaning up the dishes, her family retired, except for Nate. When he turned to make a laughing remark, she had gone to her room and no amount of calling at the door brought more response than, "Goodnight, Nate. I'll tell you everything tomorrow."

Crouched on her bed in the fluffy gown, Rose waited an eternity until the ranch house lay still. Then her cold fingers struggled with fastenings and she removed her birthday dress. She even carefully hung it up, conscious of the expense her parents had gone to so she would be pleased. Maybe someday she would be able to wear it without feeling those strong arms around her. She shuddered and forced the memory away, pulling on her jeans and shirt. She added a warm jacket and her sombrero and carried her boots.

Step by step she descended the stairs like a wraith. She had no plan in mind, no firm destination. She could never overtake Mike Carey and, even if she did, how much respect would he have for a girl who led a man on until he felt his kiss would be welcomed, even returned?

Armed against the cold night with warm clothing and the sting of hot shame, Rose quickly saddled Mesquite. She admonished him to silence and led him across the carpet of leaves under the cottonwoods before mounting. Even then she kept him to a walk until the range stretched before them in the moonlight. Now she could safely call in his ear and thrill to his smooth swift gait, and perhaps put to rest memories too painful to bear.

TWELVE

Mike Carey rode away from the Double B angry, depressed, and disillusioned. How could the girl he had grown to love allow a man such as Dan Sharpe to hold her close? Even in the pale moonlight there had been no mistaking the way the dark and white figures merged. Darkness and light, purity and innocence against evil.

Why had he ever come to Wyoming, anyway? The lure of now-dimmed dreams had captured him and now mocked him. Should he ride back to the Circle 5 and pack his gear, head to Rock Springs, and catch the first train back to Concord?

"Never!" The word rang in the still night. What kind of man was he to give up just because Desert Rose Birchfield had fallen from the pedestal where he had placed her? She wasn't all of Wyoming. He loved the mountains and valleys, the rushing streams and wildflowers, the vivid leaves and cold mornings as if he had been born among them. Besides, a kiss didn't mean Dan Sharpe had put his brand on Rose. Mike's jaw set. He hadn't hung around to see what happened after the kiss. . . .

"Whoa, Peso." He reined in so sharply his horse snorted. What a fool he had been. Perhaps Rose could have used his help if Sharpe had kissed her without her consent. He almost turned back then laughed harshly. Too late now to retrace his steps and charge back to the ranch like a knight in armor. Neither could he be sure his chivalry was needed.

For several minutes Mike and Peso stood statuelike in the trail before moving on toward the Circle 5. Yet in those minutes the distant sound of hooves increased in volume until Mike knew someone galloped toward him from the Double B. Probably Joe, come to find him. Nate would have told Joe how abruptly he left the party.

Mike impulsively guided Peso off the trail and into the deep black shelter of a clump of nearby trees. He couldn't talk to Joe now. "Quiet, Peso," he whispered when the singing hooves drew near. The next moment Mike straightened in the saddle, his mouth hanging open. The rider wasn't Joe Perkins but Dan Sharpe, grim-faced in the moonlight and riding an already lathered horse as if death and destruction chased him.

What did it mean? Puzzlement gave way to glee. No happy sweetheart rode away like that. Rose must have rejected the foreman's advances. Relief nearly unseated Mike. He waited until Sharpe disappeared over a hill before riding back to the trail. His boss didn't look to be in a mood for company. More like a mood for murder. Mike's hands convulsively tightened on the reins. All the distrust he had felt since arriving on the Circle 5 rose in a surge of suspicion and he hurried Peso along, always keeping far enough behind Sharpe to escape detection. Even when the foreman heard hooves he'd assume it was some of the hands going home from the party.

Peso trotted up a hill that gave a view of the trail ahead. Mike couldn't believe his eyes. As far as he could see, that trail lay empty in the moonlight! Of all the strange things. Mike blinked and stared again. No movement ahead. A chill crawled down his spine. Had Sharpe discovered someone following him and taken cover to ambush the rider?

Don't be an idiot, Mike told himself. He jerked his gaze from the trail and quickly examined both sides of the valley through which it ran. Mike took in a deep breath.

A buckskin and rider appeared on the edge of the section of land between Hardwick's Lazy H and the Double B, *the same land where Joe Perkins had been shot that night weeks ago.*

"All right, old man, we'd better find out what's going on." Mike tethered Peso instead of letting the reins hang loose. Slipping and sliding in his dress shoes, he longed for the heavy boots he usually wore but hadn't stopped to change into when he hastily left the party. After a dozen steps he took precious time from his pursuit and raced to his saddlebags and changed. In those seconds Sharpe gained distance, although he had slowed his horse's pace considerably. Mike ran from cover to cover and when Sharpe pulled in the buckskin, he found refuge in a prickly bush to the ruin of his dress suit.

The clear air carried sounds perfectly and Mike lay prone, listening with all his might.

"That you, boss?" An unfamiliar voice called.

"Who are you expecting? The governor?" Sharpe's voice showed his vile mood and Mike raised his head and parted the bushes so he could see. He almost gave himself away when Sharpe started flinging off his dress suit and white shirt then stepped into work clothing and carelessly stuffed his good clothes into his saddlebag. Last of all, Sharpe tied a bandana across his face just under his eyes and pulled his big hat low. "Ready?"

Four similarly clad men, complete with bandana masks, circled Sharpe. One demanded, "What took you so blasted long? We gotta get these cattle outa here before yore hands start home."

"Keep your shirt on," Sharpe barked. "Miss Desert Rose Birchfield's party will last for hours yet."

Mike gritted his teeth and prayed for help. He passionately wanted to leap out of hiding and smash Sharpe's face for the way he said Rose's name.

"Haw, haw, guess it will at that. Well, let's get on with it." The clatter of hooves and creak of leather slowly faded. Mike sat up and rubbed his eyes. Had he really seen five masked men sitting there planning a night raid of Hardwick's cattle? "Ouch!" He rubbed his hand. Both the prickly bush and the incredible scene were real. The question now was, what should he do? Ride back to the Double B for help? The whole Hardwick crew was at the party.

Mike deliberated. Five men against one

offered odds only overcome in adventure novels. Trying to hold up the holdup men would be insane. What if he tracked them so he could find out where they took the rustled cattle? Could he do it?

"I have to," he muttered. "If I go get help it will mean shooting and killing. If I can identify the men then find the cattle the law will get them."

His heart thumped, anticipating the long night ahead. He climbed the hill back to Peso, sighed with regret that he still wore the suit, and stepped into the saddle. "Old man, Carmichael Blake-Jones never in his wildest imagination pictured anything like this." He chuckled. "Wonder what Mercy will say when I write to her about it? She'll probably wish she'd been here with me!"

Hours later Mike wearily tailed the five riders and about thirty head of cattle they hazed off toward the mountains. Shock chased away his fatigue when he saw Sharpe's chosen path — across the edge of the Double B not far below the knoll where Mike first saw Desert Rose. The fickle moon darted in and out of gathering clouds, casting eerie shadows on the sinister scene.

Five minutes later raindrops spattered the earth. Mike threw on the slicker he'd learned always to keep rolled behind his saddle. It concealed his dress suit as well, with his pant legs stuffed into his high boot tops. If he were spotted, he could pass as one of the riders. He took further precautions by searching his saddlebags for a neckerchief and knotting it around his neck. He'd observed in following the rustlers that once they left the section of land with their stolen cattle the men pulled down their masks but left them handy.

"Hey boss, someone's comin'!" a hoarse voice warned. Mike froze and strained to hear. Above the slow-moving shuffle of cattle came the clear, rhythmic sound of hooves.

"Get your masks on and keep the cattle moving," Sharpe called. "I'll take care of the jasper. Probably a night herder."

The moon chose that moment to reveal the exciting happenings below. Mike stifled a cry when he saw the gun in Sharpe's hand. He wheeled, still unobserved. He must cut off the unsuspecting rider before Sharpe got to him.

Too late. Peso with all his skill couldn't intercept the racing roan. . . .

"Please God, no!" Mike whispered, unable to tear his gaze from Mesquite, carrying Desert Rose into danger at a dead run.

A hiss from Sharpe betrayed his fury.

"You!" He snatched the bandana mask from his face.

"What are you doing on our land and with our cattle?" Rose's voice rang like a hammer on an anvil. Mesquite slid to a stop.

Sharpe doffed his hat. "They aren't your cattle. They were Hardwick's but they're mine now."

"You beast!" She raised her quirt and struck him full in the face.

Sharpe's gun spat and the bullet sped past Rose within inches. "That's the second time tonight you've struck me. It won't happen again." He kept the gun trained on her. "I'll shoot to kill if I have to." His eyes glittered. "That shouldn't be necessary, however. I have other plans for you. Strange how history really does repeat itself, only this time the ending will be different."

Rose fearlessly challenged him. "You know you will be found out and hanged this time, as you would have been before if Mother and Aunt Ivy hadn't kept still."

Mike saw the powerful convulsion of Sharpe's shoulders. "So they broke their word and told after all."

"They did not!" Rose's voice went to a high pitch. "Nate accidentally overheard them talking and he told me."

Sharpe shrugged. "Just as well. Now,

young lady, you're going with us." The gun pointed steady while he dismounted.

"I am not! I won't tell if you'll let me go." For the first time she betrayed her fear.

"Moffatt, get over here," Sharpe ordered at the top of his lungs and one of the four men with the herd rode back. "Tie her to the saddle and blindfold her."

Moffatt grunted. "I never bargained for nothin' like this." Obviously reluctant he obeyed but only after spirited resistance from Rose.

"I won't gag you if you promise not to holler," Sharpe told the bound girl just before Moffatt wrapped a scarf over her eyes that blazed hate at her captors.

"Why should I holler when there's no one around?" she burst out and squirmed helplessly against the ropes. "I'm not stupid, Dan Sharpe."

He cursed. "Shut up. The first noise out of you and you're gagged. Moffatt, put her horse on a lead line behind mine then halt the cattle." His teeth gleamed. "Miss Birchfield and I will ride ahead so any tracks will be stamped out by our new herd."

Mike felt sweat crawl under his collar. Only the knowledge he could be of better help to the girl by remaining undiscovered held him from taking his chances and holding up Sharpe and Moffatt. *Keep cool,* a little voice inside commanded. *It's your — and her — only chance.*

Bad as things were, they got worse. Sleet that chilled and washed out tracks fell until Mike's hands turned numb. Misery washed over him. Yet the faith of his childhood that had returned since he reached Wyoming routed total despair. Surely God would make a way. Mike clung to this thought and kept his distance from the herd and riders ahead.

Dawn streaked gray and the rain had turned to snow before Sharpe's trek ended. The exhausted men and cattle had been led across rocky patches, down slopes and up trails Sharpe must have learned by heart. Mike had thought he knew the country from combing the draws for wandering cattle, but he'd never come across the sheltered valley hidden deep in the mountains like a pocket in a cloak. To his amazement a snug cabin awaited the riders, old but in good repair. How he longed to warm himself at the crackling fire Moffatt built that sent smoke curling into the snowstorm! Shivering outside an uncurtained back window, Mike noticed the snow had increased until it had already filled the tracks behind them. How could he survive if he remained? Yet could he bear to leave Desert Rose here with this gang of outlaws, especially the ruthless Dan Sharpe?

He crept away from the cabin and stamped life back into his hands and feet. Taking advantage of the heavy snowfall, he even dared to build a tiny fire. If the rustlers smelled smoke they'd associate it with their own fire. Next to the trunk of a large spruce the snow barely sifted through the tightly interlaced branches and Mike managed to sleep.

He awakened to take stock of the situation. The best thing he could do was abduct Rose and get her away, soon. Threat of another storm offered possible protection. Everything would depend on how things lay in the cabin. Mike crept back to his post and rejoiced. Rose lay on a bunk just inside the window to the left, concealed from the main part of the cabin by an old blanket someone had strung up.

At least she hadn't been mistreated or she wouldn't sleep so soundly. He wormed his way around the cabin and pressed his ear to the crack in the door. At the first words he heard he clenched his hands and set his teeth into his lower lip.

"I'm agin it." Moffatt's glare matched the looks on other faces. "Forcin' a girl like her to marry's a pure shame, an' kidnappin's likely to get us hung."

Sharpe's ugly laugh made the hair rise on the back of Mike's neck. "Once I've married her it won't be kidnapping but elopement. Wives can't testify against their husbands."

"Count me out." Moffatt spat into the open fireplace with its blazing logs. His grizzled countenance turned toward the silent three grouped near the fire. "Me an' the boys'll be ridin' out soon as the snow quits for sure. You can send us our share when you sell the critters." His suggestion carried the weight of an order. "I wouldn't advise any funny business neither."

"Oh, you'll get your money. You always have, haven't you?" Sharpe rolled a cigarette, lit it, and puffed out a cloud of smoke that hid his face.

"There never was a skirt mixed up in our dealin's before," Moffatt reminded.

"By all that's holy, I didn't ask her to stick her nose in." Sharpe leaped to his feet so fast his rude chair crashed to the floor. "Now that she has, I'm going to marry her and even old scores."

"And just how do you plan to do that?" a new voice demanded. A tanned hand shoved back the frail curtain partition and Desert

Rose Birchfield stepped toward the men. "It takes a minister to marry folks and somehow I just can't see Uncle Nat taking kindly to performing a ceremony for us."

Magnificent! Mike wanted to shout. The sleep had given Rose new courage and strength.

Evidently Sharpe's men thought so too for Moffatt laughed and the others joined in.

"Shut up, all of you!" Dan Sharpe glared at his men then at Rose. "Justices of the peace marry folks, too, and I just happen to know one not more than two miles from here due east."

"You're lying," Rose laughed scornfully. "No decent justice of the peace would be holed up out here in the winter unless —"

"Unless he is a rascal who needed to get away," Sharpe finished smoothly. "I'd rather have married you in the proper way than have a rascally man read the lines but then circumstances don't always allow for all the nicer things in life."

"And you think such a ceremony will hold? When the moment we get back to civilization I'll tell what really happened?" Rose laughed in Sharpe's face. "You must be mad."

Sharpe's tawny eyebrows rose almost to

his hairline. "You turned eighteen yesterday, my dear girl. With both my justice of the peace friend and myself swearing this is an elopement and that you left the Double B and came after me of your own free will, we'll be married proper and binding."

Rose whirled toward the other men and cried, "You're going to let him get away with this?"

Moffatt shrugged and the others shifted uneasily. "We didn't ask to get in on this an' we're agin it but we're ridin' out soon as we can. This other ain't none of our business."

"You — you —" Sheer fury cut off her indictment and Rose ran back behind her curtain and pulled it into place.

Weak from holding himself back, Mike slunk away. Not until he could trust himself to speak rationally did he dare creep back to the little window. Rose sat huddled on the bunk, all the fight she had shown earlier gone. Mike tapped gently, then again. She turned. Hope replaced fear in her glorious eyes. She glanced at the curtain then imperiously waved Mike away from the window and opened it a crack.

"What are you doing in there?" Sharpe bellowed.

"Getting some fresh air," she yelled back. "Who can stand all the smoke?" She defiantly pushed the window up more.

"Don't get any ideas about trying to run away from your bridegroom-to-be," Sharpe taunted. "On foot in the snowstorm that's coming you'd get maybe fifty feet." He laughed delightedly.

Mike reached for the two hands she held out to him. "Quick, don't ask questions. Can you slip out after they're asleep?"

Her cheeks whitened. "I'll try, but if they catch you —"

"They won't. God will help us." He saw color return but she clung to his hands.

"Mike, you're here, you're involved?"

"I can't explain now. If you start out and anyone challenges you, tell them you're going to the — the —"

"I understand." Her eyes looked enormous. "Where will I find you?"

"I'll be watching." He pressed her hands, smiled, and fled into the safety of the woods.

Endless hours later when the early November dark had come, Mike stood by Peso, ready and waiting. No danger of discovery now. The expected snow had come again and the large lazy flakes showed every intention of multiplying and continuing for hours. The glow from the fire that had streamed through the window earlier dwindled. Silence replaced the occasional laugh and sporadic conversation. Still Mike waited.

The cabin door opened. A bundled-up figure stepped onto the porch, silhouetted against the dimly lit interior.

"Where are you going?" Sharpe's voice followed.

"Where do you think I'm going in the middle of a snowstorm in the dark?" Rose flung back and slammed the door. She ran down the single step and into Mike's arms. He tossed her onto Peso's back in one easy motion, swung up behind her, and started off. Mesquite, whose saddle lay in the cabin, followed.

She didn't speak until they were out of earshot of the cabin. "Where are we going?"

"I've asked myself that a thousand times this afternoon," he said huskily. "We've got maybe ten minutes' start on them, the way I figure. A few minutes before they miss you, more to saddle up and find our tracks. In this snow and dark it may take some time."

"They'll expect me and whoever has me to aim straight for home." Rose shuddered. "There are so *many* of them. Do you have a gun?"

"Yes."

"Promise you won't use it unless —"

"I promise." His arms around her tightened. "Rose, if they catch us Sharpe will kill me and marry you the way he said. The others won't interfere. I'm not so sure they'll even follow us but we can't take that chance. I know this is all terrifying and I wish there were another way but if there is I just can't figure it out."

He took a deep, unsteady breath then let out a croaky little laugh. "Rose, will you go with me to that justice of the peace and marry me — tonight?"

She jerked up and Mike added, "It's for your protection. If you're already married, there's not a thing Sharpe can do about it. I doubt even he would kill me and marry my widow all at the same time."

THIRTEEN

A lifetime ago Laurel Birchfield had told her daughter, "I know that with your faith in our Heavenly Father you will never act in any way except an honorable one." Now, trapped by the storm and Dan Sharpe, Rose wondered. *Could she live up to that trust?*

Faithful Peso continued to breast the storm under a double burden. Suddenly Rose said in a broken voice, "I can't marry you, Mike, even to save my life. Marriage has to be between two persons who love each other or it can't be blessed by God."

"I have loved you ever since I saw you," Mike quietly said. "If you can't learn to care, I'll never ask anything of you except the right to protect you until I can get you back to your family."

He loved her. Mike Carey loved her. Why should the fear and gloom that closed in around them suddenly lift? Dazed, torn between an idol created through letters and a strong man who had braved both elements and man to save her, Rose's feelings churned. Carmichael Blake-Jones suddenly seemed so far away, so vague . . . she had never even seen a picture of him! Mike Carey, cowboy, was here. She thought of his golden hair, his round, appealing face, and most of all the blue eyes anyone on earth could trust. When he vowed to protect her and ask nothing in return she knew she had nothing to fear. Too tired to sort through her fears any longer, Rose shakily said, "I'll marry you."

How different she felt when Mike's arms tightened protectively around her from when Dan had pinioned her against her will! One man gave freely, expecting nothing, while the other selfishly demanded and took.

Mike's hold tightened. "I hope you will never regret it, Rose. It's the best I can do for you."

She longed to comfort him, to tell him she appreciated and cherished the dearness of him but mute lips could not form the words. Her newly awakened feelings were still too fragile and perhaps born only from the perilous situation. A little sob came but she disguised it by saying, "You — I'm not really dressed for a wedding."

"I fell in love with a girl with an auburn braid on a roan horse," he told her and again Rose marveled.

"You saw him kiss me?"

"Yes, and I ran from it. I learned what you did when out on the range Sharpe said you struck him for the *second* time." Rose felt the heat of gladness fill her veins.

Long before they reached the renegade who still carried the little justice of the peace Rose felt they had come ten miles, not two. Yet she thanked God for the ever-increasing storm. There was little likelihood that Sharpe could trail them when snow beat into their tracks and filled them quickly. Besides, why would he suspect their destination? A ripple of nervous laughter escaped and Mike's arms around her tightened.

"Are you regretting your promise, Rose?"

"No." She shivered in spite of the warmth from Mike's strong yet respectful hold. "It just isn't — I didn't think — you have to admit this isn't exactly the kind of wedding a girl imagines."

"I know." Did the husky voice whisper "dear" before Mike said, "Whatever happens, you'll be safe."

She lapsed into silence and Mike concentrated on Peso. The strong horse carrying a double load snorted and hesitated at times but picked his way when Mike wisely let the reins lie loose. A lifetime later Mike wordlessly lifted Rose from the saddle and they stamped their way to the door of a rude hut. Mike pounded and called, "Business for you, sir. We're eloping."

Eloping! Some of Rose's confusion fled but when Mike held out his hand and said, "Come," she obediently followed him into the dim interior of the hut. A quick survey in the lamplight showed it was clean. She sighed in relief and looked at the justice of the peace.

"How'd you know I lived here?" the paunchy, balding man demanded, laying a rifle on the table.

"Sharpe told me. I work on the Circle 5. Can you marry us?" Mike's voice sounded strained.

"I'll hitch you tighter than a peach and its skin," the older man bragged but turned a sharp look toward Rose.

"How old are you?"

"Eighteen."

"Names?" The justice of the peace stuck a pair of pince-nez on his nose and procured from a makeshift bureau a stubby pencil and a dirty piece of paper.

"Desert Rose Birchfield." The words had trouble getting out of her parched throat.

"Michael Carey . . ." a loud crash cut Mike off. He had backed into a chair and it overturned. "Sorry."

Rose would remember the brief ceremony only in flashes. ". . . take this man . . . love, honor . . . take this woman . . . love, honor . . ." The only words that sounded clearly in her tired brain came when Mike answered the questions with a ringing, "I do." Her own whispered responses evidently satisfied the justice of the peace for he concluded, ". . . pronounce you man and wife." He slowly removed his glasses and added, "You may kiss your bride."

Rose saw the poignant look in Mike's blue eyes before he caught her close, whispered in her ear, "We can't let him be suspicious," then tenderly, almost reverently kissed her lips.

"Sorry I can't offer honeymoon accommodations, but she can use the extra bunk and you'll have to roll up in front of the fire," their unwilling host grudgingly told them. "Night's not fit for critters, let alone humans."

"I'll take care of the horses." Mike's warning glance stilled the protest forming on Rose's lips. "We thank you." The bewildered girl admired his coolness but when he stepped out into the storm to stable Peso and Mesquite, she nearly panicked. Something in the justice of the peace's knowing look infuriated her.

"Well, Desert Rose Birchfield, eloping with a ranch hand!" He slapped his thigh and cackled. "Never thought I'd live to see it."

She summoned up every bit of ancestral southern pride to sustain her as she looked through him. "My *husband* and I appreciate your hospitality. I'm sure you will be well paid."

Greed brightened the small watching eyes and when Mike came back in and pressed money into his hand he grew positively affable. "Don't forget to sign the wedding certif'cate," he reminded.

"Go ahead, Rose. I'll just dry my coat first," Mike told her. She shakily wrote her name where the justice of the peace pointed, not reading the remarkable document. She did wonder why it took Mike so long to sign his name. Perhaps he felt as unsure as she. Too tired to care, she roasted in front of the fire until her riding jeans and shirt and socks felt dry then gratefully crept into the rough but clean blankets on the extra bunk, knowing she would never sleep. Fatigue and strain thought otherwise. Long before Mike closed his eyes and shut out the walls of the hut, Rose's soft breathing showed that she slept.

Had he done the right thing? Had his love for her prompted his bold action? Or had there been no other choice? Dear God, he prayed, and shifted on the hard floor. *Examine my heart and forgive me if I have done wrong.*

Sometime in the night the snow stopped. The Wyoming sun burst over a nearby mountain peak in a glorious flood. It first touched the tall, evergreen tree tops, then the snow-crowned roof of the shack. At last it sent an exploring finger through the single window and into the hut. Still the weary three who had been up until the early morning hours slept. Climbing higher, the sun began to melt the snow. Rose awoke when a *plop-plop* outside the window warned that the storm had passed. At the same time Mike sprang up and the justice of the peace stretched himself and muttered something inaudible.

How could he have slept so long in time of danger? Mike chastised himself and pulled on his boots. "May we trouble you for some breakfast?"

Mellowed by the generous money donation of the night before their host produced bacon, surprisingly good coffee, and a mountain of flapjacks. An hour later Mike and Rose rode away down a trail they were told was a shortcut back to the Double B, mentally making note of the location so a posse could come as soon as weather permitted. The going proved hard. Rose insisted on riding Mesquite bareback for a time but the roan's hide grew wet and slippery from kicked-up snow. Again Peso resumed his stalwart pose and carried double.

When they reached the familiar bald knob that meant home lay near, Rose's eyes filled with tears. Everything seemed so unreal. She turned to Mike and again saw the poignant blue light in his eyes that betrayed so much. "You — you promised —" She swallowed hard. "Mike, could we just keep still?" She hardly believed the look in his face. Relief? A lessening of strain?

"Whatever you say." He laid his hand over her gloved one. "It might be better not to shock your family just yet."

Rose shivered at the *just yet* but managed a wavering smile. "What shall we tell them then?"

"The truth." He acted surprised and she straightened. "Let me do the talking," he said quietly.

She numbly nodded and the horses picked their way down the slope and across the level ground to the ranch house. The warm sun had melted snow in the open and the earth felt soggy from the moisture.

"Thank God, Mike has her!" rang from Nate, who raced toward them on Piebald, his raven hair tossing wildly. "Where have you been?" He stopped his horse in front of them.

"Wait until we reach the ranch," Mike told him. "Rose is worn out and we don't want to explain but once."

A little later, warmed and fed, Rose quietly listened while Mike told her grandparents and Nate a condensed version of what had happened. "Rose decided on a midnight ride and ran into Sharpe and his band of rustlers stealing Hardwick's cattle. I happened to be trailing Sharpe and saw the whole thing. Sharpe took Rose to a cabin he must have had built for his secret meetings. I managed to get her attention and let her know I was there. She slipped out in the night and the snow covered our tracks. We found a shack for the rest of the night and came home."

"Is that all?" Nate looked at them suspiciously and acted disappointed. "We looked and looked for you but the snow defeated us."

"What more do you want?" Rose demanded. "Seems to me that cattle rustling, being abducted and carried away and rescued all in the same night should be enough for anyone, even Columbine," she mischievously added.

"I would have been scared to death," Columbine confessed, then blushed. "I — I'm sorry I ever felt sorry for Dan Sharpe!"

Rose escaped to her room in the wave of laughter that followed but not before Thomas Brown said, "Mike, are you too tired to take a ride over to Hardwick's with me?"

"Not at all." His voice floated to where Rose stood halfway up the stairs. "Except — I don't think Sharpe knows I saw him. Maybe it would be better for me to head for the Circle 5 and poke around, see if I can find anything incriminating."

"Good idea," Thomas agreed. Rose heard the stamping of his heavy boots. "Come on then, Nate."

Only after the men left did Rose realize that she hadn't even thanked Mike for saving her. Remorseful, she sprang to her window but Mike and Peso were too far away to hear her call.

All the way back to the Circle 5, Mike sternly suppressed the desire to gloat over the way things had turned out. Suppose Sharpe turned toward the justice of the peace when he could find no trace of Rose? On the other hand, why should he? The deep snow should have obliterated their tracks. Sharpe would probably think Rose had ridden off on Mesquite and headed home. Even if he did go to the justice of peace he would find no evidence of Mike Carey, unless he could get that name out of the Carmichael Blake-Jones signature Mike had used. Back and forth, back and forth his mind seesawed until he reached the corrals at the Circle 5.

"Where in tarnation have you been?" Joe Perkins, ruddier than ever, met him at the corral gate.

"Got caught out. Stayed in a shack." Should he confess to Joe who he really was? With all the intrigue and danger swirling around him, Mike knew he could use some staunch support. He searched Joe's loyal face and made a snap decision. "Come up to the ranch house with me and I'll tell you a story."

"What kind of story?" Joe followed Mike's brisk steps after Peso had been freed and rubbed down. Clinking spurs and the rolling gait of the cowboy on foot made Mike grin.

"First, we're going to search the house."

"We're *what?*" Joe gasped and his blue

eyes popped. "Are you plumb loco? If Sharpe catches us we'll be goners." He drew a brown forefinger across his throat.

Mike figuratively fired both barrels at once. "I saw Sharpe and four men steal about thirty head of Hardwick's cattle last night but it's my word against theirs. If I can find proof, bills of sale, that kind of thing, we can get him." His face hardened. "Joe, those cattle came right off that piece of land where you got shot."

Joe stuck both hands on his hips. His eyes narrowed to slits. "So—o—o, either Sharpe or one of his rustlers tried to kill me."

"Looks that way to me." They had reached the porch of the ranch house. Mike checked to see no one was around and pushed open the door. "Come on, let's get us some evidence."

"Say, I got a grudge against Sharpe but how come you're so het up to get him?" Joe demanded when their search turned up nothing.

"Keep your lip buttoned, but I own the Circle 5."

The dumbfounded cowboy stared then shoved back his hat and sadly shook his head. "Aw, now I know you're loco."

"I'm not." Mike laughed at Joe's expression. "My real name is Carmichael Carey Blake-Jones — isn't that a monicker?"

"But the owner's a Mr. Prentice," Joe argued.

"Prentice is my mother's maiden name." Mike hadn't dreamed how much fun he'd get in unmasking himself to Joe.

"One of us is crazy and it shore ain't me," Joe solemnly announced.

"Neither of us is crazy and as soon as we get this mess cleared up, how would you like to be the new Circle 5 foreman?" Mike told the dazed cowhand. He couldn't help but wickedly add, "Nice steady job, foreman. A man could think about getting married. Especially when the way I see it is, a foreman needs his privacy. I plan to build a brand-new home in the spring and there's bound to be logs and window glass enough left for a snug three- or four-room cabin over there." He waved toward a pretty knoll maybe a quarter mile from the ranch house.

"Have I died an' gone to heaven already?" Joe gasped. His mighty hand shot out and gripped Mike's. "Put her there, pard. Now how're we gonna trip up Sharpe? By the time we can get in to that little hidden valley you know he will have moved those cattle on."

"I know and I've been thinking. First

thing I'm going to do is pick a fight with our present boss when he gets back." The plan sprang full blown while he talked. "Then I'm riding into Rock Springs. I'll get myself specially deputized, come back, and seek out Sharpe's men who are getting pretty fed up with some of his doings —"

"How do you know that?" The pupils of Joe's eyes turned to steel points.

"Overheard them last night while Sharpe was holding Rose Birchfield captive."

"Wh—at?" Rage filled Joe's face and he leaped for the door.

"Hold it, she's home safe. The men wanted no part of it. What I thought I'd do was let word get around I'm for hire and not particular about what I do."

"You'll be walkin' a narrow trail," Joe warned. "Why not let me do it?" His eyes glistened.

Mike hesitated, tempted. Joe had far better skills than he. No, he wouldn't ask another man to kill his snakes.

"You lay low right here on the Circle 5 and protect my — our — interests," he ordered. "Joe, I don't have to tell you what this means to you and me and the Wyoming range."

A second strong grip of hands and they slipped out of the ranch house. Not a moment too soon, either. Joe's keen vision observed a dot in the distance and he softly laughed. " 'Pears to me, our boss is ridin' in a big hurry." He laughed again without mirth. "Reckon your chance to pick an argument's comin' quicker than you thought."

"Good." Mike's blood leaped high. "Back me, no matter what I do, all right?"

Joe only nodded but Mike had the feeling the lithe body beside him was poised to spring should it be necessary. They lounged against the corral fence until Sharpe galloped in, his face dark with anger.

"Why aren't you working?" he yelled. "I don't pay no-good hands to stand around with their hands in their pockets. Either get busy or get your time."

Mike sprang erect. "I'm taking my time, Sharpe. We've worked like slaves and you know it. Well, no more. Are you coming with me, Joe?" He shot a secret glance of warning toward Joe who glanced down and drew circles in the ground with his boot. "Well, are you?"

"Uh, sorry, but I reckon I'll stick." Apology shone in the blue eyes and Mike had to look back toward Sharpe to conceal his gleam of triumph.

"Of all the — I thought we were pards."

Mike worked himself into a simulated rage. He took off his sombrero and threw it on the ground. "This Circle 5's one fine place!"

"That's enough," Sharpe barked. His face fairly shouted his glee over finally getting rid of the cowboy who had been a burr under his saddle ever since he rode in. "Pack your gear and get out, Carey. You'll have what's coming to you ready by the time you are." He dismounted and tossed his buckskin's reins to Joe. "Rub him down, Perkins."

"I don't know if I can stick it," Joe burst out the moment Sharpe got out of hearing distance. "With you gone, the boss will treat me lower than Wyomin' dirt." He sighed. "Just don't make it too long, pard. I mean, boss."

"Just pard," Mike told him and noticed how Joe smiled in relief. "One other thing. If we meet in town, don't act too friendly and be sure and drop some hints here and there on how funny I've been acting. Wonder out loud if I'm guilty of something nobody knows and that's why I've gone back on you."

"Aw, Mike, I can't do that!" Joe protested. "At least, not to the Birchfields."

"You have to or we'll never get Sharpe." Mike walked toward the bunkhouse and softly reminded, "Everything will work out but a lot rides on how well you play your part." An hour later he rode into Antelope and acted out the disgruntled jobless cowboy to perfection. After staying overnight, he headed for Rock Springs, thankful for the continuing fair weather that had followed the snowstorm.

A week later he returned, properly deputized and eager to put Sharpe back behind bars. From the frosty glares he received Mike knew Joe had done his work well. Word reached Mike that Sharpe had boldly ridden to the Double B and called on Desert Rose, blandly assuring the Browns and Nate he had found the girl injured from a fall and so delirious she thought she was being abducted. Sharpe even offered to bring in his men to verify the story and only shrugged when Rose turned on him and said he lied, but refused to allow her parents to take action against him. Mike realized she must be protecting him and he prayed for self-control to carry out his work.

FOURTEEN

One winter afternoon shortly before Christmas Rose sought out Nate and led him to a quiet room away from the Browns. "Nate, I've heard rumors about Mike Carey. What do you know?" She watched him with eyes made keen by torment.

Nate started to speak then closed his lips in a straight line. When he finally opened them again he only said, "What have you heard?"

Cold fear settled in Rose's heart. "That time he rescued me, I've never been able to figure out why he happened to be there." She restlessly pleated the fine blue wool of her gown. "Now range gossip has it that Mike's quit the Circle 5, is drifting and —"

"I can't talk about it," Nate cut in, looking like a thunderhead. "Say, what do you hear from your traveling friend?"

Rose looked down at her nervous fingers. "I — we won't be writing again. Things were getting out of hand so I told him it would be best to break off our correspondence."

She didn't add as she could have done that the decision came after tears and prayers. If she relinquished something fine and wonderful, yet the God who had helped her so many times sent the courage to tell the truth. A few days after she came back to the Double B she wrote to Carmichael Blake-Jones and told him she had married and wouldn't be writing again. She thanked him for his many pleasant letters and said how much she appreciated them. She didn't tell him that if what she suspected were true, her shadowy husband wasn't the Christian cowboy she thought him but in all probability a rustler.

"Is that the letter you gave me to mail?" Nate asked in a choked voice and hid his face in his hands.

"Yes. I know you admire him a lot and I do — did too."

"But I remember bringing you a letter from him after that," Nate protested, his head still down.

Rose almost blurted out the whole story but bit her tongue. She simply couldn't explain without telling about her marriage. Rose fervently hoped Michael wouldn't mention it in a letter to Nate! She replied, "Yes, he wrote once."

"What did he say?" Nate appeared to be holding his breath.

Tired of deceit, Rose went as far as she could. "He said I had broken his heart. That he fell in love with me when he saw my picture." She glared at her cousin. "See what you started? That's not all. Do you know who Mr. Carmichael Blake-Jones is?" She didn't wait for Nate's answer but excitedly went on. "He's also Mr. Prentice, the new owner of the Circle 5, *and he expects to take over and run the ranch.* Probably in the spring. Oh, dear, what am I going to do?" A hated tear fell and she angrily brushed it away.

A curious blend of amusement, concern, and pity made Nate's face a closed book and he patted her arm. "I have a feeling that in time everything will work out just fine, Rosy. Wish I could be here to see it." Disappointment vanished when he squared his shoulders and smiled. "Oh well, the sooner I go and learn what I must the quicker I can come back and serve our Lord."

Rose put away her own troubles. Yet when Nate left her depression came. She had to tell her parents of the hasty marriage and before Carmichael Prentice or whatever his name really was came, but how could she, now that Mike might have turned to rustling? Had he? She couldn't believe it. Range rumors had to be wrong and this aching sense of loss merely a test of her loyalty. The last thing she needed was Michael's arrival to complicate things even more.

Christmas passed. Nate swung aboard the eastbound train, leaving Rose desolate. Without her cousin or Michael's letters she fell prey to her own thoughts. Columbine and Sam offered companionship when they weren't in school but long winter hours stretched and lengthened into January and February. Rose alternated between excitement when Nate's scrawled letters came, filled with boyish admiration for a girl named Mercy Curtis, to melancholy. Her infrequent glimpses of Mike Carey helped little.

Mike seldom came to church and Dan Sharpe seldom missed. Sharpe seemed impervious to slanted stares and whispers from other ranchhands. Hardwick, Nate, Thomas Brown, and the others who had gone to the little valley found trampled ground when the snows lifted but no evidence. Sharpe continued his way unhampered. Sometimes Rose, who had chosen to spend most of the winter on the Double B, saw a biding-my-time look in Grandpa Brown's eyes when Sharpe's name came up. At least the winter wasn't one of the worst. Rose and Mesquite could get out at times into the snow-hardened paths and clear, cold days.

"Whatever happened to that nice Mike Carey who used to come over?" Grandma innocently asked one morning at breakfast.

Rose steadied her fork with shaking fingers. "He doesn't work for the Circle 5 anymore."

"Land sakes, how young folks do hop around!" Grandma's keen eyes sparkled. "I'm sorry to hear it. He seemed such a nice, steady young man, not at all like some of our good-hearted but rough boys."

Grandpa cut in with an irrelevant remark and Rose wondered how much or what he had heard but didn't dare ask. Yet she couldn't avoid overhearing the growing whispers concerning Mike Carey, now viewed by much of the range as a man of mystery.

Finally spring arrived and bestowed a mixed blessing. April's mercurial outlook reflected Rose's own up-and-down moods. Memory of her marriage ceremony dimmed until at times she felt it had happened to someone else. Now and then she saw Mike at a distance when she went out riding but he never approached her. "Probably ashamed to," she told Mesquite after one such occurrence. The thought plummeted her spirits even further and it took a mile of galloping with the wind in her face to regain her composure.

Driven by doubt and a growing love for her absent husband that Rose at last could deny no longer, she decided she must know for sure Mike Carey's true character. He had risked danger, saved Columbine and then herself. Still, he *had* been right there with Sharpe and his rustlers and if the latest rumors could be believed, Mike had actually been seen riding with some of the worst ruffians in Wyoming just a few weeks before.

Rose had consistently resisted riding near the Circle 5 but one bright morning when Columbine and Sam clamored for her to go with them she consented.

"You won't believe the *gorgeous* house going up over there," Columbine told her. "A second house, actually a big log cabin, is being built just a little way off." Red streaked her fair skin. "Last time Sam and I went the workers were just putting in huge windows. You can see the mountains and hills and valley. What a wonderful place to live."

Sam drawled in his own comical way. "Reckon it could be arranged. Someone said Sharpe's getting ready to leave. If you can charm the new owner, Columbine, the house and view go with him."

A rush of emotion made Rose hastily bend down to check her stirrup. *I hope Columbine has better luck with men than I. First, I have too many in my life and now no one. Mike must have changed his mind, and of course I couldn't keep on writing to Michael.* The thought hurt and made her lash out, "I hope you haven't been over here running after Joe Perkins, Columbine."

Her sister's pretty chin tilted up. "I don't have to run after Joe or any man. He isn't even here when we ride over. He's out with the cattle." Tears burned her eyes at the unjust accusation. "Just because you've moped ever since Nate left doesn't mean you have to act so mean to me." She touched her horse's flanks with her heels and shot ahead.

Sam gave her a look of reproach that clearly told how Rose's own hopes for a close relationship between him and Columbine had come to pass. "She's right, you know." He loped ahead as well.

Rose felt sick and disgusted with herself. "Wait," she called and goaded Mesquite into a gallop. "I'm sorry, Columbine." Even though her sister promptly forgave her, Rose couldn't forget the stricken look in her eyes or the way Sam had responded. Things simply couldn't go on this way. Better to set off an explosion than to keep all her misery bottled up inside.

Three days later the terrible feeling of waiting ended. Rose overheard her grandfather, Hardwick, and several other ranchers discussing a cattle raid planned for that night. Someone had leaked the news, perhaps in the Pronghorn or Silver saloon or to a friend who promptly reported it to the sheriff. "This is our chance to get the whole gang," Hardwick snapped and closed his big hand in a significant gesture. "If the report is true the rustlers are going for every head of cattle they can get away with then move out of Wyoming pronto."

"Call in every decent man you can get," Thomas Brown ordered. "Leave only enough hands with the herds so the rustlers won't get suspicious and tell them not to resist. We don't want dead cowboys. The cattle aren't worth that. Pass the word that we'll meet here at ten o'clock tonight."

Rose slipped away, her heart frozen. An

inner sense told her Mike Carey would be in the midst of the rustler gang tonight. "He must not," she whispered under her breath and at the same moment flung herself outdoors and to the corral. Her fingers made short work of saddling up and a few minutes later she and Mesquite began their quest to find and stop Mike while time remained.

All during the long winter and early spring Mike's conscience warred with duty. He had sworn to uphold the right but could God approve of the way he had chosen? A dozen times he considered abandoning the entire scheme, heartily sick of deception and ashamed of the final letter he impulsively wrote to Rose. Not that every word wasn't true. He realized his first sight of her in the photograph had intrigued him and the clear eyes innocently beckoned him. *Would she ever forgive him?* Nate said yes when they had a long talk. Outside of the justice of the peace only Nate knew of the marriage one snowy December night. Mike had gone back and further insured the man's silence with a large sum of money. Whether he could be trusted remained to be seen. The gathering storm was bound to break soon and sweep away the need for secrecy. After that. . . . At this point Mike refused to consider the future.

His role of disgruntled cowboy, sore at Sharpe, brought in rich dividends. Once after griping how Sharpe had ridden him so hard he couldn't stomach working for the Circle 5 foreman, a disreputable, slouching cowboy approached him. Moffatt, the man who had balked over Sharpe's forced elopement, hinted broadly that he knew a way to get even with Sharpe. A few sessions later Mike learned Moffatt and the others had never been paid for the cattle they rustled from Hardwick.

"Can't understand it," Moffatt confessed. "He always paid up before. This time he keeps sayin' it's too dangerous." He barked a short laugh. "Why's one time dangerouser than another?" He leaned close and confidentially whispered, "I think he's hooked on that Birchfield gal and gettin' even. He won't even let us move those critters from where he's hid them. Says we'll make one more grand raid and clear out." His eyes gleamed. "I figure he's goin' to doublecross us so we're aimin' to get to the cattle first. Hardwick and Brown and some of the other ranchers are on spring roundup right now. We'll let them get the cows all collected for us then mosey out and start movin' them, the night before Sharpe's big raid."

Mike almost choked in an effort to hide his exultation.

"Are you with us?" Moffatt demanded.

"I'll be there." Mike emphatically shook on it. Under the cloak of darkness Mike dispatched a note to the sheriff warning him of the raid. Being discovered now had no part in his plan.

Only one flaw appeared in the carefully set up trap: Dan Sharpe's absence. Mike thought about it then smiled and wrote a second note.

YORE BEING DOUBLE XED. RAID TO-MORROW NIGHT.

He signed it, *A friend,* then rode out and found Joe Perkins and told him to get the message to Sharpe but not let him know who delivered it. Joe's eyes gleamed with the prospect of action. "I reckon there's goin' to be some mighty surprised fellers," he said.

"I just hope we can get away without any shooting," Mike told him soberly. Joe looked wise and replied, "It all d'pends on how surprised everyone is."

The next day Mike stayed in town at Moffatt's direction. The rustler said, "Keep your eyes open and mouth shut." Mike wanted to laugh; the advice echoed his Rock Springs lawyer's statement exactly. Yet the impending events made Mike restless. He walked up and down the streets for a time then saddled Peso and rode out toward the Double B as he had done a hundred times in the past few months. Every time the truth had trembled on his lips only to be bitten back. No one, not even Desert Rose Birchfield Blake-Jones, must know his plan. One careless word could destroy all he had worked so hard to set up.

Spring with all its shades of green softened the range. Mike and Peso climbed to the bald knob overlook and Mike dismounted. The drumming of hooves warned him but it was too late. Before he could remount and ride off, Rose and Mesquite topped the rise and slid to a stop.

"Hello, Rose." Mike had no choice but to remain strong at all cost.

Her face pale in spite of her fast ride, she slid from the saddle. "I came to find you." She stepped close and clutched his arms with strong hands. Her fearless dark eyes gazed into his. "Once you said you loved me. Is it still true?"

"It is." He didn't move a muscle.

"Then ride away from Antelope and don't stop until Peso gives out." Her words fell like small icicles into the late afternoon.

"I can't."

Her self-control broke. "You must!" she cried. "Don't you know what happens to rustlers? You'll spend years in jail. Mike, you said you loved God. If you won't leave for my sake, will you go for His?"

A passing cloud dimmed the sun's increasing rays. Birds hushed their songs. Mike could only shake his head.

Rich color replaced her pallor but her steady and searching gaze never left his face. "I'll go with you if you'll go now."

He jerked back as if struck. "You'd do that for me? Why?"

"I can't bear to have you turn from God and be dishonorable." Her long eyelashes drooped and so did her shoulders. Her nerveless hands fell from his arms.

"Why should it matter so much to you?" Mike's head spun. "Why, Rose?" he repeated but she didn't answer.

With a magnificent toss of her head she stepped back and demanded, "What difference does it make? Isn't it enough that I will go with you? I'm your wife." She paled again and her dark eyes grew enormous.

"You would sacrifice yourself to save me," Mike marveled. For one mad moment he almost gave in. To ride away with Rose offered the strongest temptation he had ever known. Only his inner call to a trait passed down from Puritan ancestors, duty, stopped him. He caught her hands in his. "I'd give everything on earth to do what you ask, my darling, but I can't." He felt the shudder that rocked her body.

"Rose, dearest, trust me for a little longer. I swear before God I am not doing anything wrong or wicked. Will you believe me and go back to the Double B?"

She stared at him and Mike saw the awful struggle within her soul. Seconds crawled into minutes but at last she whispered, "I trust you."

With a triumphant cry he encircled her with his arms and kissed her as he would have liked the night they married. Then he tore himself free, led Mesquite close, and waited until Rose mounted. "I promise you will never regret your trust," he told her. "Very soon I can explain everything."

She lifted the reins but he laid one hand on the pommel. "Rose, are you learning to care?"

Her sweet lips trembled. She patted his hand then removed it from the pommel. Not until Mesquite danced away with her did she reply in a low call that thrilled Mike to his boots. "Perhaps." Her laughing face turned rosy. She waved and rode away, leaving him shaken and thanking God.

Hours later Rose paced her room. She had come back to the Double B as Mike asked but she never promised to stay there. A quick look out the window revealed dark forms gathering in the starlight. Fear clutched the watching girl's throat. She could not bear the long night of waiting. The moment the riders started, she slipped downstairs to where she had tied Mesquite, already saddled, and mingled with the others. Her sombrero and the heavy coat of her grandfather's she had donned effectively hid her identity. Only her wildly beating heart threatened to betray her.

The surprise Joe mentioned worked in the posse's favor. Moffatt and his men had no suspicions and rode practically into the arms of the posse whose presence paralyzed them.

Hardwick's stentorian, "Hands up or we'll shoot!" and the zing of well-placed lassos rid the range of the outlaws who had plagued ranchers for months.

"Well, just see who's here!" Thomas Brown whirled toward the big buckskin that had dashed into the circle of men around the prisoners.

"I want every one of these men and Mike Carey arrested for rustling," Dan Sharpe's voice boomed out. "I've been watching them for weeks and —"

"You don't leave us holdin' the gunnysack," Moffatt bellowed. "Me and my men'll take our medicine but we ain't standin' by while you get away with it." A string of profanity followed. "Sheriff, Sharpe's behind us. We'd akept still if he'd paid us like he promised. Now he can go to jail along with the rest of us and Carey."

"Carey?" The sheriff glanced at Mike, rigid in the starlight.

Joe Perkins stepped down from his pinto Splotch and faced Sharpe. "My pard ain't no rustler an' never has been. He was sworn in as a special dep'ty months ago, on purpose to stop this here stealin' of yours."

A gasp ran through the crowd of men. Sharpe's jaw sagged then he reached for his revolver. "Liar! You're in this, too, and I'm going to. . . ."

"Go, Peso!" Mike spurred on his quarter horse. Peso's flying leap knocked Sharpe flat. He cursed, aimed, and fired. Mike felt a hard blow in his chest and slumped in the saddle.

Released from their stupor by the shot, a dozen men piled onto Sharpe with Joe Perkins going first. Willing hands hauled Mike from the saddle. Barely conscious, his last thought was, I fought the good fight and kept the faith. Then, blackness pierced only by a girl's scream. . . .

While stories of his heroism swept the valley, Mike Carey lay fighting for his life. All the skill Adam Birchfield possessed, the power of special prayer meetings on Mike's behalf, and Desert Rose's refusal to let him go combined in a mighty effort. Day and night Rose hovered close by. When alone on watch, she let the love in her heart overflow and clung to her husband's hands, willing him to live.

Five days after the shooting, Adam took his daughter aside. "He's very near the crisis. If he lives through the night he has a slim chance."

"He isn't going to die." Wan but determined, Rose proudly lifted her tired head.

"Would you have his suffering go on and on?" Adam asked and stroked his daughter's auburn braid.

Rose shook her head as she clung to her father. Yet for hours she prayed Mike might be spared. Not until he sighed deep in his coma, his face waxen, could Rose come to the point where she changed her prayer. "Thy will, Lord, not mine." Better for his suffering to end and hers to go on. She rested her head on his pillow, so weary she could no longer hold it up. Adam found her there an hour later.

"Rose." He gently shook her awake.

She lifted heavy, tear-swollen eyelids. "Is he gone?"

"No, praise God. He's sleeping naturally. Now you must rest." He held out his arms and she flew into their comfort after a quick confirming look at their patient. A few minutes later she fell into a deep, untroubled sleep and didn't awaken until early evening. Adam warned her not to stay long now that Mike had begun the long trail back. He must not talk.

So Rose only said when he opened his eyes, "You were shot. Everything is over and you're going to be better."

Satisfied, he slept again while his body healed. When Rose came into the room, his gaze never left her. Something in his look disturbed her, a shadow she couldn't describe. He said little about the fight except to express gladness the rustlers and Sharpe had been sent to prison. He never mentioned their encounter on the bald knob.

Not until the end of May would Adam pronounce Mike fit enough to ride. The shadow in his eyes grew deeper. Even the welcome news that Nate would be coming soon did not erase it. "Will you ride with me?" he asked when Adam agreed to a short outing.

"Of course." Rose couldn't understand why her heart pounded so at the prospect of a mere ride. They didn't go clear to the bald knob but to a secluded spot by a rushing stream where the cottonwoods seemed to whisper their secrets.

"Rose," Mike began after they seated themselves on a big rock.

"Will you tell me about Carmichael Blake-Jones, please?"

"Nate told you!" Misery made her stammer. "It was a dare and I never meant any harm. I feel so ashamed." She bit her lip and stared at the churning water feeling tossed like the leaves that fell and whirled downward.

"Nate says he owns the Circle 5 and intends to run it. Are you in love with him?" Mike shifted position.

"No." She turned and met the blue gaze fixed on her. "Once I thought I might be." She couldn't continue.

He gently took her hand and the poignant light she loved filled his eyes. "Then would plain Mike Carey, the man you married, have a chance at capturing your heart?"

False pride faded. Too many hours of

certainty and fear had driven it away. "Yes, Mike." She courageously continued to look straight into his face.

"Whoopee!" Mike roared. He dropped her hands, threw his hat into the air, and jumped until she wondered if he had gone mad.

"Stop, stop, Mike. Dad would never have let you come if he'd known you wouldn't be careful. What's wrong with you?" She sprang to her feet only to be caught and swung around. "Mike, stop it. What possesses you?"

"I have a confession too. My full name is Carmichael Carey Blake-Jones." Mischief danced in his every movement.

"You!" Desert Rose wondered if she had heard right. "Then, all this time. . . ." Her voice stumbled over her rising anger.

"I never lied to you, Rose. I just didn't tell all the truth. I promise never to deceive you again." He held her away from him. "I also want you to know that I would never have agreed to Nate's prank if I hadn't fallen in love with your photograph."

"But you didn't have a photograph when I wrote the advertisement," she protested, too stunned by the revelation to make sense of it.

"Nate sent your letter directly to me with

one enclosed."

"How he must have crowed," she said bitterly and jerked free. "I hate being made a fool of and that's what you've done."

The same poignant blue light returned. "Desert Rose, far from it. The more I got to know the wonderful girl, the more I hated the underhanded way I met her. Won't you forgive me?" Spent from the exertion, he laughed unsteadily. "I think I'd better sit down again." He seated himself crosslegged on the ground, his face suddenly pale.

Rose's anger vanished forever with a rush of memories that brought back those desperate hours when she saw Mike fading in spite of all she could do. Now she threw herself down and confessed, "When I knew Carmichael Blake-Jones would live in the new home on the Circle 5 I felt jealous of the girl he would marry even though by then I knew I loved a cantankerous cowboy named Mike Carey."

His kiss silenced her. Then Mike pointed toward the mountains. "Soon the snows will be gone from the peaks, probably about the time Nate comes. The wildflowers will be gorgeous. We must finish supervising the building on the Circle 5 now, but God willing, would my wife like a camping honeymoon a little later?"

Rose felt her throat tighten at the prospect. "She would." She stayed quiet within his arms for a moment then said, "Michael, do you think God planned this all along? I could forgive Nate better if I thought that."

"God certainly knew it would happen," he soberly told her. "If I had known just a year ago what a harvest I would reap —" His arms tightened. "There's still a harvest of souls waiting and what better way to gather them than by Christian living and example? We're just links in the strong chain of His followers who have been given a white field. Our children and grandchildren must be taught the only happiness is in serving our Lord and Master."

"They will be," she assured and rested her head on his shoulder. "If God can take the thorns from a desert rose, He will surely guide us." She gently freed herself, stood, and held out her tanned hand. "Come, we must go home." Hand in hand they walked toward Peso and Mesquite and began their life's journey together.

Mercy Curtis never kept house for her uncle but she did come to Wyoming a year later. As Mrs. Nate Birchfield she put to good use all the housewifely skills she had culti-vated. She and Columbine Perkins joined

Rose in the many tasks pioneer and ranch women performed that helped their husbands proclaim the good news of the Gospel of Jesus Christ. Sam followed in Dr. Adam Birchfield's footsteps as a medical doctor while Nate and Reverend Nat Birchfield tended to the souls of the Wind River Range.

ABOUT THE AUTHOR

Colleen L. Reece is a prolific author with over sixty published books. With the popular *Storm Clouds over Chantel,* Reece established herself as a doyenne of Christian romance.